Cesar's Wife

A Comedy in Three Acts

W. Somerset Maugham

Cesar's Wife: A Comedy in Three Acts

The present edition is a reproduction of previous publication of this classic work. Minor typographical errors may have been corrected without note, however, for an authentic reading experience the spelling, punctuation, and capitalization have been retained from the original text.

ISBN: 978-1-61895-973-7

CONTENTS

CHARACTERS

Sir Arthur Little, K.C.B., K.C.M.G.

Ronald Parry.

Henry Pritchard.

Richard Appleby, M.P.

Osman Pasha

Violet

Mrs. Etheridge.

Mrs. Pritchard.

Appleby

An English Butler; Native Servants; an Arab Gardener

The scene is laid in Cairo, in the house and garden of the British Consular Agent.

ACT I

Scene: The morning-room in the Consular Agent's house at Cairo. The windows are Arabic in character and so are the architraves of the doors, but otherwise it is an English room, airy and spacious. The furniture is lacquer and Chippendale, there are cool chintzes on the chairs and sofas, cut roses in glass vases, and growing azaleas in pots; but here and there an Eastern antiquity, a helmet and a coat of mail, a piece of woodwork, reminds one of the Mussulman conquest of Egypt; while an ancient god in porphyry, graven images in blue pottery, blue bowls, recall an older civilisation still.

When the curtain rises the room is empty, the blinds are down so as to keep out the heat, and it is dim and mysterious. A Servant comes in, a dark-skinned native in the gorgeous uniform, red and gold, of the Consular Agent's establishment, and draws the blinds. Through the windows is seen the garden with palm-trees, oranges and lemons, tropical plants with giant leaves; and beyond, the radiant blue of the sky. In the distance is heard the plaintive, guttural wailing of an Arab song. A Gardener in a pale blue gaberdine passes with a basket on his arm.

Servant.

Es-salâm 'alêkum (Peace be with you).

Gardener.

U'alêkum es-Salâm warahmet Allâh wa barakâta (And with you be peace and God's mercy and blessing).

[The Servant goes out. The Gardener stops for a moment to nail back a straggling creeper and then goes on his way. The door is opened.
Appleby comes in with Anne Etheridge and they are followed

2

immediately by Violet Anne is a woman of forty, but handsome still, very pleasant and sympathetic; she is a woman of the world, tactful and self-controlled. She is dressed in light, summery things. Appleby is an elderly, homely woman, soberly but not inexpensively dressed. The wife of a North-country manufacturer, she spends a good deal of money on rather dowdy clothes. Violet is a very pretty young woman of twenty. She looks very fresh and English in her muslin frock; there is something spring-like and virginal in her appearance, and her manners of dress is romantic rather than modish. She suggests a lady in a Gainsborough portrait rather than a drawing in a paper of Paris fashions. Luncheon is just finished and when they come in the women leave the door open for the men to follow.]

Mrs. Appleby.

How cool it is in here! This isn't the room we were in before lunch?

Anne.

No. They keep the windows closed and the blinds drawn all the morning so that it's beautifully cool when one comes in.

Mrs. Appleby.

I suppose we shan't feel the heat so much when we've been here a few days.

Anne.

Oh, but this is nothing to what you'll get in Upper Egypt.

Violet.

[*As she enters.*] Is Mrs. Appleby complaining of the heat? I love it.

Anne.

Dear Violet, wait till May comes and June. You don't know how exhausting it gets.

Violet.

I'm looking forward to it. I think in some past life I must have been a lizard.

Mrs. Appleby.

I dare say the first year you won't feel it. I have a brother settled in Canada, and he says the first year people come out from England they don't feel the cold anything like what they do later on.

Anne.

I've spent a good many winters here, and I always make a point of getting away by the fifteenth of March.

Mrs. Appleby.

Oh, are you staying as late as that?

Anne.

Good gracious, no. You make Lady Little's heart positively sink.

Violet.

Nonsense, Anne, you know we want you to stay as long as ever you can.

Anne.

I used to have an apartment in Cairo, but I've given it up now and Lady Little asked me to come and stay at the Agency while I was getting everything settled.

Mrs. Appleby.

Oh, then you knew Sir Arthur before he married?

Anne.

Oh, yes, he's one of my oldest friends. I can't help thinking Lady Little must have great sweetness of character to put up with me.

Violet.

Or you must be a perfect miracle of tact, darling.

Mrs. Appleby.

My belief is, it's a little of both.

Anne.

When Arthur came to see me one day last July and told me he was going to marry the most wonderful girl in the world, of course I thought good-bye. A man thinks he can keep his bachelor friendships, but he never does.

Mrs. Appleby.

His wife generally sees to that.

Violet.

Well, I think it's nonsense, especially with a man like Arthur who'd been a bachelor so long and naturally had his life laid out before ever I came into it. And besides, I'm devoted to Anne.

Anne.

It's dear of you to say so.

Violet.

I came here as an absolute stranger. And after all, I wasn't very old, was I?

Mrs. Appleby.

Nineteen?

Violet.

Oh, no, I was older than that. I was nearly twenty.

Mrs. Appleby.

[*Smiling.*] Good gracious!

Violet.

It was rather alarming to find oneself on a sudden the wife of a man in Arthur's position. I was dreadfully self-conscious; I felt that everybody's eyes were upon me. And you don't know how easy it is to make mistakes in a country that's half Eastern and half European.

5

Anne.

To say nothing of having to deal with the representatives of half a dozen Great Powers all outrageously susceptible.

Violet.

And, you know, there was the feeling that the smallest false step might do the greatest harm to Arthur and his work here. I had only just left the schoolroom and I found myself almost a political personage. If it hadn't been for Anne I should have made a dreadful mess of things.

Anne.

Oh, I don't think that. You had two assets which would have made people excuse a great deal of inexperience, your grace and your beauty.

Violet.

You say very nice things to me, Anne.

Mrs. Appleby.

Your marriage was so romantic, I can't see how anyone could help feeling very kindly towards you.

Violet.

There's not much room for romance in the heart of the wife of one of the Agents of the foreign Powers when she thinks she hasn't been given her proper place at a dinner party.

Mrs. Appleby.

I remember wondering at the time whether you weren't a little overcome by all the excitement caused by your marriage.

Violet.

I was excited too, you know.

Mrs. Appleby.

Everyone had always looked upon Sir Arthur as a confirmed

bachelor. It was thought he cared for nothing but his work. He's had a wonderful career, hasn't he?

Violet.

The Prime Minister told me he was the most competent man he'd ever met.

Anne.

I've always thought he must be a comfort to any Government. Whenever anyone has made a hash of things he's been sent to put them straight.

Violet.

Well, he always has.

Mrs. Appleby.

Mr. Appleby was saying only this morning he was the last man one would expect to marry in haste.

Violet.

Let's hope he won't repent at leisure.

Anne.

[*Smiling.*] Mrs. Appleby is dying to know all about it, Violet.

Mrs. Appleby.

I'm an old woman, Lady Little.

Violet.

[*Gaily.*] Well, I met Arthur at a week-end party. He'd come home on leave and all sorts of important people had been asked to meet him. I was frightened out of my life. The duchesses had strawberry leaves hanging all over them and they looked at me down their noses. And the Cabinet Ministers' wives had protruding teeth and they looked at me up their noses.

Anne.

What nonsense you talk, Violet!

7

Violet.

I was expecting to be terrified of Arthur. After all, I knew he was a great man. But you know, I wasn't a bit. He was inclined to be rather fatherly at first, so I cheeked him.

Anne.

I can imagine his surprise. No one had done that for twenty years.

Violet.

When you know Arthur at all well you discover that when he wants anything he doesn't hesitate to ask for it. He told our hostess that he wanted me to sit next to him at dinner. That didn't suit her at all, but she didn't like to say no. Somehow people don't say no to Arthur. The Cabinet Ministers' wives looked more like camels than ever, and by Sunday evening, my dear, the duchesses' strawberry leaves began to curl and crackle.

Anne.

Your poor hostess, I feel for her. To have got hold of a real lion for your party and then have him refuse to bother himself with anybody but a chit of a girl whom you'd asked just to make an even number!

Mrs. Appleby.

He just fell in love with you at first sight?

Violet.

That's what he says now.

Mrs. Appleby.

Did you know?

Violet.

I thought it looked very like it, you know, only it was so improbable. Then came an invitation from a woman I only just knew for the next week-end, and she said Arthur would be there. Then my heart really did begin to go pit-a-pat. I took the letter in to my sister and sat on her bed and we talked it over. "Does he mean to propose to me," I said, "or does he not?" And my sister said: "I can't imagine what he sees in you. Will you accept him if he does?" she asked. "Oh, no," I said. "Good heavens, why he's twenty years older than I am!" But of course I meant to all the time. I shouldn't have cared if he was a hundred, he was the most wonderful man I'd ever known.

Mrs. Appleby.

And did he propose to you that week-end, when he'd practically only seen you once before?

Violet.

I got down in the afternoon and he was there already. As soon as I swallowed a cup of tea he said: "Come out for a walk." Well, I'd have loved a second cup, but I didn't like to say so, so I went. But we had a second tea in a cottage half an hour later, and we were engaged then.

[Appleby *comes in with* Osman Pasha. Mr. Appleby *is a self-made man who has entered Parliament; he is about sixty, grey-bearded, rather short and stout, with some accent in his speech, shrewd, simple and good-natured. He wears a blue serge suit.* Osman Pasha *is a swarthy, bearded Oriental, obese, elderly but dignified; he wears the official frock-coat of the Khedivial service and a tarbush.*]

Appleby.

Sir Arthur is coming in one moment. He is talking to one of his secretaries.

Violet.

Really, it's too bad of them not to leave him alone even when he's snatching a mouthful of food.

Osman Pasha.

Vous permettez que j'apporte ma cigarette, chère Madame.

Violet.

Of course. Come and sit here, Pasha.

9

Appleby.

I wanted to tell his Excellency how interested I am in his proposal to found a technical college in Cairo, but I can't speak French.

Violet.

Oh, but his Excellency understands English perfectly, and I believe really he talks it as well as I do, only he won't.

Osman Pasha.

Madame, je ne comprends l'anglais que quand vous le parlez, et tout galant homme sait ce que dit une jolie femme.

Anne.

[*Translating for the* Applebys.] He says he only understands English when Lady Little speaks it, and every nice man understands what a pretty woman says.

Violet.

No one pays me such charming compliments as you do. You know I'm learning Arabic.

Osman Pasha.

C'est une bien belle langue, et vous, madame, vous avez autant d'intelligence que de beauté.

Violet.

I have a Copt who comes to me every day. And I practise a little with your brother, Anne.

Anne.

[*To* Mrs. Appleby.] My brother is one of Sir Arthur's secretaries. I expect it was he that Mr. Appleby left with Sir Arthur.

Violet.

If it is I shall scold him. He knows quite well that he has no right to come and bother Arthur when he's in the bosom of his family. But they say he's a wonderful Arabic scholar.

Osman Pasha.

Vous parlez de M. Parry? Je n'ai jamais connu un Anglais qui avait une telle facilité.

Anne.

He says he's never known an Englishman who speaks so well as Ronny.

Violet.

It's a fearfully difficult language. Sometimes my head seems to get tied up in knots.

[*Two* Saises *come in, one with a salver on which are coffee cups and the other bearing a small tray on which is a silver vessel containing Turkish coffee. They go round giving coffee to the various people, then wait in silence. When* Sir Arthur *comes in they give him his coffee and go out.*]

Anne.

It's wonderful of you to persevere.

Violet.

Oh, you know, Ronny's very encouraging. He says I'm really getting on. I want so badly to be able to talk. You can't think how enthusiastic I am about Egypt. I love it.

Osman Pasha.

Pas plus que l'Égypte vous aime, Madame.

Violet.

When we landed at Alexandria and I saw that blue sky and that coloured, gesticulating crowd, my heart leapt. I knew I was going to be happy. And every day I've loved Egypt more. I love its antiquities, I love the desert and the streets of Cairo and those dear little villages by the Nile. I never knew there was such beauty in the world. I thought you only read of romance in books; I didn't know there was a country where it sat by the side of a well under the palm-trees, as though it were at home.

Osman Pasha.

Vous êtes charmante, madame. C'est un bien beau pays. Il n'a besoin que d'une chose pour qu'on puisse y vivre.

Anne.

[*Translating.*] It's a beautiful country. It only wants one thing to make it livable. And what is that, your Excellency?

Osman Pasha.

La liberté.

Appleby.

Liberty?

[Arthur *has come in when first* Violet *begins to speak of Egypt and he listens to her enthusiasm with an indulgent smile. At the Pasha's remark he comes forward.* Arthur Little *is a man of forty-five, alert, young in manner, very intelligent, with the urbanity, self-assurance, tact, and resourcefulness of the experienced diplomatist. Nothing escapes him, but he does not often show how much he notices.*]

Arthur.

Egypt has the liberty to do well, your Excellency. Does it need the liberty to do ill before it loses the inclination to do it?

Violet.

[*To* Mrs. Appleby.] I hope you don't mind Turkish coffee?

Mrs. Appleby.

Oh, no, I like it.

Violet.

I'm so glad. I think it perfectly delicious.

Arthur.

You have in my wife an enthusiastic admirer of this country, Pasha.

12

Osman Pasha.

J'en suis ravi.

Arthur.

I've told Ronny to come in and have a cup of coffee. [*To* Anne.] I thought you'd like to say how d'you do to him.

Anne.

Are you very busy to-day?

Arthur.

We're always busy. Isn't that so, Excellency?

Osman Pasha.

En effet, et je vous demanderai permission de me retirer. Mon bureau m'appelle.

[*He gets up and shakes hands with* Violet.]

Violet.

It was charming of you to come.

Osman Pasha.

Mon Dieu, madame, c'est moi qui vous remercie de m'avoir donné l'occasion de saluer votre grâce et votre beauté.

[*He bows to the rest of the company.* Arthur *leads him towards the door and he goes out.*]

Anne.

You take all these compliments without turning a hair, Violet.

Arthur.

[*Coming back.*] You know, that's a wonderful old man. He's so well-bred, he has such exquisite manners, it's hard to realise that if it were possible he would have us all massacred to-morrow.

13

Appleby.

I remember there was a certain uneasiness in England when you recommended that he should be made Minister of Education.

Arthur.

They don't always understand local conditions in England. Osman is a Moslem of the old school. He has a bitter hatred of the English. In course of years he has come to accept the inevitable, but he's not resigned to it. He never loses sight of his aim.

Appleby.

And that is?

Arthur.

Why, bless you, to drive the English into the sea. But he's a clever old rascal, and he sees that one of the first things that must be done is to educate the Egyptians. Well, we want to educate them too. I had all sorts of reforms in mind which I would never have got the strict Mohammedans to accept if they hadn't been brought forward by a man whose patriotism they believe in and whose orthodoxy is beyond suspicion.

Anne.

Don't you find it embarrassing to work with a man you distrust?

Arthur.

I don't distrust him. I have a certain admiration for him, and I bear him no grudge at all because at the bottom of his heart he simply loathes me.

Appleby.

I don't see why he should do that.

Arthur.

I was in Egypt for three years when I was quite a young man. I was very small fry then, but I came into collision with Osman and he tried to poison me. I was very ill for two months, and he's never forgiven me because I recovered.

14

Appleby.

What a scoundrel!

Arthur.

He would be a little out of place in a Nonconformist community. In the good old days of Ismael he had one of his wives beaten to death and thrown into the Nile.

Appleby.

But is it right to give high office to a man of that character?

Arthur.

They were the manners and customs of the times.

Mrs. Appleby.

But he tried to kill you. Don't you bear him any ill will?

Arthur.

I don't think it was very friendly, you know, but after all no statesman can afford to pay attention to his private feelings. His duty is to find the round peg for the round hole and put him in.

Anne.

Why does he come here?

Arthur.

He has a very great and respectful admiration for Violet. She chaffs him, if you please, and the old man adores her. I think she's done more to reconcile him to the British occupation than all our diplomacy.

Mrs. Appleby.

It must be wonderful to have power in a country like this.

Violet.

Power? Oh, I haven't that. But it makes me so proud to think I can be of any use at all. I only wish I had the chance to do more. Since I've been here I've grown very patriotic.

[Ronald Parry *comes in. He is a young man, very good-looking, fresh and pleasant, with a peculiar charm of manner.*]

Arthur.

Ah, here is Ronny.

Ronny.

Am I too late for my cup of coffee?

Violet.

No, it will be brought to you at once.

Ronny.

[*Shaking hands with* Violet.] Good morning.

Violet.

This is Mr. Parry. Mr. and Mrs. Appleby.

Ronny.

How d'you do?

Arthur.

Now, Ronny, don't put on your Foreign Office manner. Mr. and Mrs. Appleby are very nice people.

Mrs. Appleby.

I'm glad you think that, Sir Arthur.

Arthur.

Well, when you left your cards with a soup ticket from the F.O. my heart sank.

Appleby.

There, my dear, I told you he wouldn't want to be bothered with us.

16

Arthur.

You see, I expected a pompous couple who knew all about everything and were going to tell me exactly how Egypt ought to be governed. A Member of Parliament doesn't inspire confidence in the worried bosom of a Government official.

Violet.

I don't know if you think you're putting Mr. and Mrs. Appleby at their ease, Arthur.

Arthur.

Oh, but I shouldn't say this if I hadn't been most agreeably disappointed.

Mrs. Appleby.

I never forget the days when Mr. Appleby used to light the kitchen fire himself and I used to do the week's washing every Monday morning. I don't think we've changed much since then, either of us.

Arthur.

I know, and I'm really grateful to the Foreign Office for having given you your letter.

Mrs. Appleby.

It's been a great treat to us to come and see you. And it's done my heart good to see Lady Little. If you don't mind my saying so she's like a spring morning and it makes one glad to be alive just to look at her.

Violet.

Oh, don't!

Arthur.

I'm inclined to feel very kindly to everyone who feels kindly towards her. You must enjoy yourselves in Upper Egypt and when you come back to Cairo you must let us know.

Appleby.

I'm expecting to learn a good deal from my journey.

Arthur.

You may learn a good deal that will surprise you. You may learn that there are races in the world that seem born to rule and races that seem born to serve; that democracy is not a panacea for all the ills of mankind, but merely one system of government like another, which hasn't had a long enough trial to make it certain whether it is desirable or not; that freedom generally means the power of the strong to oppress the weak, and that the wise statesman gives men the illusion of it but not the substance—in short, a number of things which must be very disturbing to the equilibrium of a Radical Member of Parliament.

Anne.

On the other hand, you'll see our beautiful Nile and the temples.

Arthur.

And perhaps they'll suggest to you that however old the world is it's ever young, and that when all's said and done the most permanent on the face of the earth is what seems the most transitory—the ideal.

Appleby.

Fanny, it looks to me as though we'd bitten off as big a piece of cake as we can chew with any comfort.

Mrs. Appleby.

Oh, well, we'll do our best. And though I never could do arithmetic I've always thought perhaps one might be saved without. Good-bye, Lady Little, and thank you for having us.

Violet.

Good-bye.

[*There are general farewells and they go to the door.* Ronny *opens it for them. They go out.*]

Ronny.

I forgot to tell you, sir, Mrs. Pritchard has just telephoned to ask if she can see you on a matter of business.

Arthur.

[*With a grim smile.*] Say I'm very busy to-day, and I regret exceedingly that it will be quite impossible for me to see her.

Ronny.

[*With a twinkle in his eye.*] She said she was coming round at once.

Arthur.

If she's made up her mind to see me at all costs she might have saved herself the trouble of ringing up to find out if it was convenient.

Anne.

Your sister is a determined creature, Arthur.

Arthur.

I know. I have some authority in the affairs of this country, but none over dear Christina. I wonder what she wants.

Violet.

Let us hope for the best.

Arthur.

I've noticed that whenever anyone wants to see me very urgently it's never to give me anything. When Christina wants to see me urgently my only safety is in instant flight.

Violet.

You must be nice to her, Arthur. If you're not she'll only take it out of me.

Arthur.

It's monstrous, isn't it?

Violet.

After all, she kept house for you for ten years. Admirably, mind you.

Arthur.

Admirably. She has a genius for order and organisation in the house. Everything went like clockwork. She never wasted a farthing. She saved me hundreds of pounds. She led me a dog's life. I've come to the conclusion there's nothing so detestable as a good housekeeper.

Violet.

How fortunate you married me, then! But you can't expect her to see that point of view. It's very hard for her to be turned out of this very pleasant billet, and it's natural that when you won't do something she asks you she should put it down to my influence.

Anne.

It must have been a very difficult position for you.

Violet.

I did all I could to make her like me. I did feel rather like a usurper, you know. I tried to make her see that I didn't at all want to put on airs.

Arthur.

Fortunately she's taken it very well. I confess I was a little nervous when she told me she meant to stay on in Egypt to be near her son.

Anne.

It would be a detestable person who didn't like Violet, I think.

Arthur.

Detestable. I should have no hesitation in having him deported.

Ronny.

I think I'd better be getting back to my work.

Anne.

Oh, Ronny, would you like me to come and help you with your packing?

Violet.

[*To* Ronny.] Are you going somewhere?

Ronny.

I'm leaving Cairo.

Anne.

Didn't you know? Ronny has just been appointed to Paris.

Violet.

Is he going to leave Egypt for good?

[*She is taken aback by the news. She clenches her hand on the rail of a chair;* Arthur *and* Anne *notice the little, instinctive motion.*]

Ronny.

I suppose so.

Violet.

But why was it kept from me? Why have you been making a secret of it?

Arthur.

Darling, no one's been making a secret of it. I—I thought Anne would have told you.

Violet.

Oh, it doesn't matter at all, but Ronny has been in the habit of doing all sorts of things for me. It would have been convenient if I'd been told that a change was going to be made.

Arthur.

I'm very sorry. It was only arranged this morning. I received a telegram from the Foreign Office. I thought it would interest Anne, so I sent Ronny along to tell her.

Violet.

I hate to be treated like a child.

[*There is a moment's embarrassment.*]

Anne.

It was stupid of me. I ought to have come and told you. I was so pleased and excited that I forgot.

Violet.

I don't quite know why you should have been so excited.

Anne.

It will be very nice for me to have Ronny so near. You see, now I've given up my flat I shan't come to Egypt very often and I should never have seen Ronny. I can run over to Paris constantly. Besides, it's a step, isn't it? And I want to see him an Ambassador before I die.

Violet.

I don't see what good it will do him in Paris to speak Arabic like a native.

Arthur.

Oh, well, that is the F.O. all over. The best Persian scholar in the Service has spent the last six years in Washington.

Ronny.

It's been a great surprise for me. I expected to remain in Egypt indefinitely.

Violet.

[*Recovering herself.*] I expect you'll have a very good time in Paris. When do you go?

22

Ronny.

There's a boat the day after to-morrow. Sir Arthur thought I'd better take that.

Violet.

[*Scarcely mistress of herself.*] As soon as that! [*Recovering, gaily.*] We shall miss you dreadfully. I can't imagine what I shall do without you. [*To* Anne.] You can't think how useful he's been to me since I came here.

Ronny.

It's very kind of you to say so.

Violet.

He's invaluable at functions and things like that. You see, he knows where everyone should sit at dinner. And at first he used to coach me with details about various people so that I shouldn't say the wrong thing.

Arthur.

If you had you'd have said it so charmingly that no one would have resented it.

Violet.

I'm so afraid that the man who takes Ronny's place will refuse to write my invitations for me.

Arthur.

It's not exactly the duty of my secretaries.

Violet.

No, but I do hate doing it myself. And Ronny was able to imitate my handwriting.

Arthur.

I'm sure he could never write as badly as you.

23

Violet.

Oh, yes, he could. Couldn't you?

Ronny.

I managed to write quite enough like you for people not to notice the difference.

Violet.

You know, there are thirty-two invitations to do now.

Anne.

Why don't you send cards?

Violet.

Oh, I think a letter is so much more polite. Somehow I don't feel old enough to ask people to dine with me in the third person.

Ronny.

I'll come and do them the moment Sir Arthur can let me go.

Arthur.

You'd better do them before Violet goes out.

Violet.

That'll be very soon. The Khedive's mother has asked me to go and see her at half-past three. I'll get the list now, shall I? I don't think I'll wait for Christina. If she wants to see you on business I dare say she'd rather I wasn't there.

Arthur.

Very well.

Violet.

[*To* Ronny.] Will you come here when you're ready?

Ronny.

Certainly.

[*She goes out.*]

24

Arthur.

Have you finished that report yet?

Ronny.

Not quite, sir. It will be ready in ten minutes.

Arthur.

Put it on my desk.

Ronny.

All right, sir.

[*Exit.* Arthur *and* Anne *are left alone. He looks at her reflectively.*]

Arthur.

Violet is very sensitive to anything that might be considered a slight.

Anne.

It's very natural, isn't it? A high-spirited girl.

Arthur.

She likes me to tell her my arrangements. It gives her a little feeling of importance to know things before other people.

Anne.

Oh, of course. I quite understand. I should do the same in her place.

Arthur.

I ought to have remembered and told her that Ronny was going. She was just a little vexed because she thought I'd been fixing things up behind her back.

Anne.

Yes, I know. It would naturally put her out for a moment to learn on a sudden that one of the persons she'd been thrown in contact with was going away.

Arthur.

[*With a twinkle in his eye*.] I'm wondering if I must blame you for the loss of an excellent secretary.

Anne.

Me?

Arthur.

I don't know why the F.O. should suddenly have made up their minds that your brother was wanted in Paris. Have you been pulling strings?

Anne.

[*Smiling*.] What a suspicious nature you have!

Arthur.

Anne, own up.

Anne.

I thought Ronny was getting into a groove here. There didn't seem to be much more for him to do than he has been doing for some time. If you *will* have the truth, I've been moving heaven and earth to get him moved.

Arthur.

How deceitful of you not to have said a word about it!

Anne.

I didn't want to make him restless. I knew he'd be mad to go to Paris. I thought it much better not to say anything till it was settled.

Arthur.

D'you think he's mad to go to Paris?

Anne.

[*Fencing with him*.] Any young man would be.

Arthur.

I wonder if he'd be very much disappointed if I made other arrangements.

Anne.

What do you mean, Arthur? You wouldn't prevent him from going when I've done everything in the world to get him away.

Arthur.

[*Abruptly.*] Why should you be so anxious for him to go?

[*She looks at him for an instant in dismay.*]

Anne.

Good heavens, don't speak so sharply to me. I told Violet just now. I wanted him to be more get-at-able. I think he stands a much better chance of being noticed if he's in a place like Paris.

Arthur.

[*With a smile.*] Ah, yes, you said you were coming less frequently to Egypt than in the past. It might be worth while to keep Ronny here in order to tempt you back.

Anne.

Egypt isn't the same to me that it was.

Arthur.

I hope my marriage has made no difference to our friendship, Anne. You know how deeply I value it.

Anne.

You used to come and see me very often. You knew I was discreet and you used to talk over with me all sorts of matters which occupied you. I was pleased and flattered. Of course I realised that those pleasant conversations of ours must stop when you married. I only came here this winter to collect my goods and chattels.

Arthur.

You make me feel vaguely guilty towards you.

Anne.

Of course you're nothing of the sort. But I don't want Violet to feel that I am making any attempt to—to monopolise you. She's been charming to me. The more I know her the more delightful I find her.

Arthur.

It's very nice of you to say so.

Anne.

You know I've always had a great admiration for you. I'm so glad to see you married to a girl who's not unworthy of you.

Arthur.

I suppose it was a dangerous experiment for a man of my age to marry a girl of nineteen.

Anne.

I think one can admit that. But you've always been one of the favourites of the gods. You've made a wonderful success of it.

Arthur.

It needs on a husband's part infinite tact, patience, and tolerance.

Anne.

You have the great advantage that Violet is genuinely in love with you.

Arthur.

I suppose only a fatuous ass would confess that a beautiful girl was in love with him.

Anne.

You make her very happy.

Arthur.

There's nothing I wouldn't do to achieve that. I'm more desperately in love with Violet even than when I first married her.

Anne.

I'm so glad. *I* want nothing but your happiness.

Arthur.

Here is Christina.

[*The door opens as he says these words and an English Butler ushers in* Mrs. Pritchard. *She is a tall, spare woman, with hair turning grey, comely, upright in her carriage, with decision of character indicated by every gesture; but though masterful and firm to attain her ends, she is an honest woman, direct, truthful and not without humour. She is admirably gowned in a manner befitting her station and importance.*]

Butler.

Mrs. Pritchard.

[*Exit.*]

Arthur.

I knew it was you, Christina. I felt a sense of responsibility descend upon the house.

Christina.

[*Kissing him.*] How is Violet?

Arthur.

Lovely.

Christina.

I was inquiring about her health.

Arthur.

Her health is perfect.

Christina.

At her age one's always well, I suppose. [*Kissing* Anne.] How d'you do? And how are you, my poor Arthur?

Arthur.

You ask me as though I was a doddering old gentleman, crippled with rheumatism. I'm in the best of health, thank you very much, and very active for my years. [Christina *has seen a flower on the table that has fallen from a bowl, and picks it up and puts it back in its place.*] Why do you do that?

Christina.

I don't like untidiness.

Arthur.

I do.

[*He takes the flower out again and places it on the table.*]

Christina.

I was expecting to find you in your office.

Arthur.

Do you think I'm neglecting my work? I thought it more becoming to wait for you here.

Christina.

I wanted to see you on a matter of business.

Arthur.

So I understood from your message. I feel convinced you're going to put me in the way of making my fortune.

Anne.

I'll leave you, shall I?

Christina.

Oh, no, pray don't. There's not the least reason why you shouldn't hear what it's all about.

Arthur.

You're not going to make my fortune after all. You're going to ask me to do something.

Christina.

What makes you think that?

Arthur.

You want a third person present to be witness to my brutal selfishness when I refuse. I know you, Christina.

Christina.

[*Smiling.*] You're much too sensible to refuse a perfectly reasonable request.

Arthur.

Let us hear it. [*She sits down on the sofa. The cushions have been disordered by people sitting on them and she shakes them out, and pats them and arranges them in their place.*] I wish you'd leave the furniture alone, Christina.

Christina.

I cannot make out what pleasure people take in seeing things out of their proper place.

Arthur.

You're very long in coming to the point.

Christina.

I hear that the Khedive has quarrelled with his secretary.

Arthur.

You're a marvellous woman, Christina. You get hold of all the harem gossip.

31

Christina.

It's true, isn't it?

Arthur.

Yes. But I only heard of it myself just before luncheon. How did it come to your ears?

Christina.

That doesn't matter, does it? I have a way of hearing things that may be of interest to me.

Arthur.

I'm afraid I'm very dense, but I don't see how it can be of any particular interest to you.

Christina.

[*Smiling.*] Dear Arthur. The Khedive has asked you to recommend him an English secretary.

Anne.

Has he really? That's a change. He's never had an English secretary before.

Arthur.

Never.

Anne.

It's a wonderful opportunity.

Arthur.

If we get the right man he can be of the greatest possible help. If he's tactful, wise, and courteous, there's no reason why in time he shouldn't attain very considerable influence over the Khedive. If we can really get the Khedive to work honestly and sincerely with us, instead of hampering us by all kinds of secret devices, we can do miracles in this country.

Anne.

What a splendid chance for the man who gets the job!

32

Arthur.

I suppose it is. If he has the right qualities he may achieve anything. And after all, it's a splendid chance to be able to render such great service to our own old country.

Christina.

Has the Khedive given any particulars about the sort of man he wants?

Arthur.

He naturally wants a young man and a good sportsman. It's important that he should be able to speak Arabic. But the qualifications which will satisfy the Khedive are nothing beside those which will satisfy me. The wrong man may cause irreparable damage to British interests.

Christina.

Have you thought that Henry would be admirably suited?

Arthur.

I can't say I have, Christina.

Christina.

He's young and he's very good at games. He speaks Arabic.

Arthur.

Quite well, I believe. I think he's very well suited to the post he has. It would be a pity to disturb him when he's just got at home with the work.

Christina.

Arthur, you can't compare a very badly paid job in the Ministry of Education with a private secretaryship to the Khedive.

Arthur.

The best job for a man is the one he's most fitted to do.

Christina.

You've got no fault to find with Henry. He's a very good worker, he's honest, industrious, and painstaking.

Arthur.

You don't praise a pair of boots because you can walk in them without discomfort; if you can't you chuck them away.

Christina.

What d'you mean by that?

Arthur.

The qualities you mention really don't deserve any particular reward. If Henry hadn't got them I'd fire him without a moment's hesitation.

Christina.

I have no doubt you'd welcome the opportunity. It's the greatest misfortune of Henry's life that he happens to be your nephew.

Arthur.

On the other hand, it's counterbalanced by his extraordinary good luck in being your son.

Christina.

You've stood in his way on every possible occasion.

Arthur.

[Good-humouredly.] You know that's not true, Christina. I've refused to perpetrate a number of abominable jobs that you've urged me to. He's had his chances as everyone else has. You're an admirable mother. If I'd listened to you he'd be Commander-in-Chief and Prime Minister by now.

Christina.

I've never asked you to do anything for Henry that wasn't perfectly reasonable.

Arthur.

It's evident then that we have different views upon what is reasonable.

Christina.

I appeal to you, Anne: do you see any objection to suggesting Henry to the Khedive as a private secretary?

Arthur.

I knew that's what she wanted you here for, Anne, to be a witness to my pig-headed obstinacy.

Christina.

Don't be absurd, Arthur. I'm asking Anne for an unprejudiced opinion.

Arthur.

Anne is unlikely to have an opinion of any value on a matter she knows nothing about.

Anne.

[*With a chuckle.*] That is a very plain hint that I can't do better than hold my tongue. I'll take it, Christina.

Christina.

It's so unreasonable of you, Arthur. You won't listen to any argument.

Arthur.

The only one you've offered yet is: here's a good job going, Henry's your nephew, give it him. My dear, don't you see the Khedive would never accept such a near relation of mine?

Christina.

I don't agree with you at all. The fact of his asking you to recommend an English secretary shows that he wants to draw the connection between you and himself closer. After all, you might give the boy a chance.

Arthur.

This is not an occasion when one can afford to give a chance. It's hit or miss. If the man I choose is a failure the Khedive will never ask me to do such a thing for him again. I can't take any risks.

Christina.

Will you tell me what qualifications Henry lacks to make him suitable for the post?

Arthur.

Certainly. It's true he speaks Arabic, but he doesn't understand the native mind. Grammars can't teach you that, my dear, only sympathy. He has the mind of an official. I often think that you must have swallowed a ramrod in early life and poor Henry was born with a foot-rule in his inside.

Christina.

I am not amused, Arthur.

Arthur.

I have no doubt in course of time he'll become a very competent official, but he'll never be anything else. He lacks imagination, and that is just as necessary to a statesman as to a novelist. Finally he has no charm.

Christina.

How can you judge? You're his uncle. You might just as well say I have no charm.

Arthur.

You haven't. You're an admirable woman, with all the substantial virtues which make you an ornament to your sex, but you have no charm.

Christina.

[*With a grim smile.*] I should be a fool if I expected you to pay me compliments, shouldn't I?

36

Arthur.

You would at all events be a woman who is unable to learn by experience.

Christina.

Besides, I don't agree with you. I think Henry has charm.

Arthur.

Why do we all call him Henry? Why does Henry suit him so admirably? If he had charm we would naturally call him Harry.

Christina.

Really, Arthur, it amazes me that a man in your position can be influenced by such absurd trifles. It's so unfair, when a boy has a dozen solid real virtues that you should refuse to recommend him for a job because he hasn't got in your opinion a frivolous, unsubstantial advantage like charm.

Arthur.

Unsubstantial it may be, but frivolous it certainly isn't. Believe me, charm is the most valuable asset that any man can have. D'you think it sounds immoral to say it compensates for the lack of brains and virtue? Alas! it happens to be true. Brains may bring you to power, but charm enables you to keep it. Without charm you will never lead men.

Christina.

And do you imagine you're likely to find a young Englishman who's a sportsman and an Arabic scholar, who has tact, imagination, sympathy, wisdom, courtesy and charm?

Anne.

If you do, Arthur, I'm afraid he won't remain here very long, because I warn you, I shall insist on marrying him.

Arthur.

It's not so formidable as it sounds. I'm going to suggest Ronny.

Christina.

[*Astounded.*] Ronald Parry! That's the very last person I should have thought you'd be inclined to suggest.

Arthur.

[*Sharply.*] Why?

Anne.

[*With dismay.*] You don't really mean that, Arthur?

Arthur.

Why not?

Christina.

[*To* Anne.] Didn't you know?

Anne.

It's the last thing that would ever have entered my head.

Christina.

I thought you'd made all arrangements for sending him away.

Arthur.

I made no arrangements at all. I received a telegram from the F.O. saying that he'd been appointed to Paris.

Anne.

[*After a very short pause.*] Don't you think you'd better leave it at that?

Arthur.

No, I don't. I'm going to wire to London explaining the circumstances and suggesting that I think him very suitable for the post that's just offered itself.

Anne.

[*Trying to take it lightly.*] I feel rather aggrieved, after all the efforts I've made to get him appointed to Paris.

Christina.

Oh, he owes that to you, does he? You thought it would be better for him to leave here?

Arthur.

[*Deliberately.*] I don't quite understand what you're driving at, Christina.

Christina.

[*Taking him up defiantly.*] I cannot imagine anyone more unsuitable than Ronald Parry.

Arthur.

That is for me to judge, isn't it?

Anne.

Perhaps the Foreign Office will say they see no reason to change their mind.

Arthur.

I don't think so.

Anne.

Have you told Ronny?

Arthur.

No, I thought it unnecessary till I'd found out whether the Khedive would be willing to take him.

Christina.

I'm amazed, Arthur. When Henry told me Ronald Parry was going I couldn't help thinking it was very desirable.

Arthur.

Why?

[*She looks at him, about to speak, then hesitates. She does not dare, and resolves to be silent. Anne comes to the rescue.*]

Anne.

Christina knows that I shall be very little in Egypt in future and how fond Ronny and I are of one another. We naturally want to be as near each other as we can.

Christina.

[*With a chuckle.*] It really amuses me that you should refuse to give a good job to Henry because you've made up your mind to give it to Ronald Parry.

[Arthur *walks up to her deliberately and faces her.*]

Arthur.

If you've got anything to say against him say it.

[*They stare at one another for a moment in silence.*]

Christina.

If you have nothing against him there's no reason why I should.

Arthur.

I see. I have a good deal to do this afternoon. If you have nothing more to say to me I'd like to get back to my work.

Christina.

Very well, I'll go.

Arthur.

You won't stop and see Violet?

Christina.

I don't think so, thank you.

[*She goes out. He opens the door for her.*]

Anne.

Why didn't you tell me just now that you'd decided to keep Ronny in Cairo?

40

Arthur.

I thought it was unnecessary till everything was settled. I daresay you'll be good enough to hold your tongue about it.

Anne.

Have you definitely made up your mind?

Arthur.

Definitely.

[*They look at one another steadily.*]

Anne.

I think I'll go up to my room. I keep to my old habit of a siesta after luncheon.

Arthur.

I wish I could get Violet to take it.

Anne.

She's so young, she doesn't feel the need of it yet.

Arthur.

Yes, she's so young.

[Anne *goes out. For a moment* Arthur *gives way to discouragement. He feels old and tired. But he hears a footstep and pulls himself together. He is his usual self, gay, gallant and humorous, when* Violet *enters the room.*]

Violet.

I saw Christina drive away. What did she want?

Arthur.

The earth.

Violet.

I hope you gave it her.

41

Arthur.

No, I'm trying to get the moon for you just now, darling, and I thought if I gave her the earth it really would upset the universe a little too much.

Violet.

I thought I'd better do these invitations before I dressed.

Arthur.

You're not going to put on a different frock to go and have tea with the Khedive's mother? You look charming in that.

Violet.

I think it's a little too young. It was all right for the morning.

Arthur.

Of course you are older this afternoon, that's quite true.

Violet.

Can you spare Ronny just now?

Arthur.

[*After an instant's pause.*] Yes, I'll send him to you at once.

Violet.

[*As he is going.*] I shall be back in time to give you your tea.

Arthur.

That will be very nice. Good-bye till then.

[*He goes out. She is meditative. She gives a slight start as* Ronny *comes in.*]

Violet.

I hope I haven't torn you away from anything very important.

Ronny.

I was only typing a very dull report. I'd just finished it.

Violet.

You mustn't ever bother about me if it's not convenient, you know.

Ronny.

I shan't have much chance, shall I?

Violet.

No.... Look, here's the list.

[*She hands him a sheet of paper on which names are scribbled, and he reads it.*]

Ronny.

It looks rather a stodgy party, doesn't it? I see you've crossed my name out.

Violet.

It's not much good asking you when you won't be here. Whom d'you advise me to ask in your place?

Ronny.

I don't know. I hate the idea of anyone being asked in my place. Shall I start on them at once?

Violet.

If you don't mind. I have to go out, you know.

[*He sits down at a writing table.*]

Ronny.

I'll start on those I dislike least.

Violet.

[*With a chuckle.*] Don't you remember when Arthur said I must ask the Von Scheidleins how we hated to write them a civil letter?

43

Ronny.

[*Writing.*] Dear Lady Sinclair.

Violet.

Oh, she asked me to call her Evelyn.

Ronny.

Hang! I'll have to start again.

Violet.

It always make me so uncomfortable to address fat old ladies by their Christian names.

Ronny.

I'll end up "yours affectionately," shall I?

Violet.

I suppose you're awfully excited at the thought of going?

Ronny.

No.

Violet.

It's a step for you, isn't it? I ... I ought to congratulate you.

Ronny.

You don't think I want to go, do you? I hate it.

Violet.

Why?

Ronny.

I've been very happy here.

Violet.

You knew you couldn't stay here for the rest of your life.

Ronny.

Why not?

Violet.

[*With an effort at self-control.*] Who is the next person on the list?

Ronny.

[*Looking at it.*] Will you miss me at all?

Violet.

I suppose I shall at first.

Ronny.

That's not a very kind thing to say.

Violet.

Isn't it? I don't mean to be unkind, Ronny.

Ronny.

Oh, I'm so miserable!

[*She gives a little cry and looks at him. She presses her hands to her heart.*]

Violet.

Let us go on with the letters.

[*Silently he writes. She does not watch him, but looks hopelessly into space. She is unable to restrain a sob.*]

Ronny.

You're crying.

Violet.

No, I'm not. I'm not. I swear I'm not. [*He gets up and goes over to*

45

her. He looks into her eyes.] It came so suddenly. I never dreamt you'd be going away.

Ronny.

Oh, Violet!

Violet.

Don't call me that. Please don't.

Ronny.

Did you know that I loved you?

Violet.

How should I know? Oh, I'm so unhappy. What have I done to deserve it?

Ronny.

I couldn't help loving you. It can't matter if I tell you now. It's the end of everything. I don't want to go without your knowing. I love you. I love you. I love you.

Violet.

Oh, Ronny!

Ronny.

It's been so wonderful, all these months. I've never known anyone to come up to you. Everything you said pleased me. I loved the way you walk, and your laugh, and the sound of your voice.

Violet.

Oh, don't!

Ronny.

I was content just to see you and to talk with you and to know you were here, near me. You've made me extraordinarily happy.

46

Violet.

Have I? Oh, I'm so glad.

Ronny.

I couldn't help myself. I tried not to think of you. You're not angry with me?

Violet.

I can't be. Oh, Ronny, I've had such a rotten time. It came upon me unawares, I didn't know what was happening. I thought I only liked you.

Ronny.

Oh, my dearest! Is it possible ...?

Violet.

And when it struck me—oh, I was so frightened. I thought it must be written on my face and everyone must see. I knew it was wrong. I knew I mustn't. I couldn't help myself.

Ronny.

Oh, say it, Violet. I want to hear you say it: "I love you."

Violet.

I love you. [*He kneels down before her and covers her hands with kisses.*] Oh, don't, don't!

Ronny.

My dearest. My very dearest.

Violet.

What have I done? I made up my mind that no one should ever know. I thought then it wouldn't matter. It needn't prevent me from doing my duty to Arthur. It didn't interfere with my affection for him. I didn't see how it could hurt anyone if I kept my love for you locked up in my heart, tightly, and it made me so happy. I rejoiced in it.

47

Ronny.

I never knew. I used to weigh every word you said to me. You never gave me a sign.

Violet.

I didn't know it was possible to love anybody as I love you, Ronny.

Ronny.

My precious!

Violet.

Oh, don't say things like that to me. It breaks my heart. I wouldn't ever have told you only I was upset by your going. If they'd only given me time to get used to the thought I wouldn't ... I wouldn't make such a fool of myself.

Ronny.

You can't grudge me that little bit of comfort.

Violet.

But it all came so suddenly, the announcement that you were going and your going. I felt I couldn't bear it. Why didn't they give me time?

Ronny.

Don't cry, my dearest, it tortures me.

Violet.

This is the last time we shall be alone, Ronny. I couldn't let you go without ... oh, my God, I can't bear it.

Ronny.

We might have been so happy together, Violet. Why didn't we meet sooner? I feel we're made for one another.

Violet.

Oh, don't talk of that. D'you suppose I haven't said to myself: "Oh, if I'd only met him first"? Oh, Ronny, Ronny, Ronny!

                        Ronny.

I never dared to think that you loved me. It's maddening that I must go. It's horrible to think of leaving you now.

                        Violet.

No, it's better. We couldn't have gone on like that. I'm glad you're going. It breaks my heart.

                        Ronny.

Oh, Violet, why didn't you wait for me?

                        Violet.

I made a mistake. I must pay for it. Arthur's so good and kind. He loves me with all his heart. Oh, what a fool I was! I didn't know what love was. I feel that my life is finished, and I'm so young, Ronny.

                        Ronny.

You know I'd do anything in the world for you.

                        Violet.

My dear one. [*They stand, face to face, looking at one another wistfully and sadly.*] It's no good, Ronny, we're both making ourselves utterly miserable. Say good-bye to me and let us part. [*He draws her towards him.*] No, don't kiss me. I don't want you to kiss me. [*He takes her in his arms and kisses her passionately.*] Oh, Ronny, I do love you so. [*At last she tears herself away from him. She sinks into a chair. He makes a movement towards her.*] No, don't come near me now. I'm so tired.

[*He looks at her for a moment, then he goes back to the table and sits down to write the letters. Their eyes meet slowly.*]

                        Ronny.

It's good-bye, then?

                        Violet.

It's good-bye.

[*She presses her hands to her heart as though the aching were unendurable. He buries his head in his hands.*]

END OF THE FIRST ACT

ACT II

The scene is the garden of the Consular Agent's residence. It is an Eastern garden with palm-trees, magnolias, and flowering bushes of azaleas. On one side is an old Arabic well-head decorated with verses from the Koran; a yellow rambler grows over the ironwork above. Rose-trees are in full bloom. On the other side are basket chairs and a table. At the bottom of the garden runs the Nile and on the farther bank are lines of palm-trees and the Eastern sky. It is towards evening and during the act the sun gradually sets.

The table is set out with tea-things. Anne is seated reading a book. The gardener in his blue gaberdine, with brown legs and the little round cap of the Egyptian workman, is watering the flowers. Christina comes in.

Anne.

[*Looking up, with a smile.*] Ah, Christina!

Christina.

I was told I should find you here. I came to see Violet, but I hear she hasn't come back yet.

Anne.

She was going to see the Khedive's mother.

Christina.

I think I'll wait for her.

Anne.

Would you like tea? I was waiting till Violet came in. I expect she's been made to eat all sorts of sweet things and she'll want a cup of tea to take the taste out of her mouth.

Christina.

No, don't have it brought for me.... I can never quite get over being treated as a guest in the house I was mistress of for so many years. [*To the Gardener.*] Imshi (Get out).

Gardener.

Dêtak sa 'ideh (May thy night be happy).

[*He goes out.*]

Anne.

Your knowledge of Arabic is rather sketchy, Christina.

Christina.

I never see why I should trouble myself with strange languages. If foreigners want to talk to me they can talk to me in English.

Anne.

But surely when we're out of our own country we're foreigners.

Christina.

Nonsense, Anne, we're English. I wonder Arthur allows Violet to learn Arabic. I can't help thinking it'll make a bad impression on the natives. *I* managed this house on fifty words of Arabic.

Anne.

[*Smiling.*] I'm convinced that on a hundred you'd be prepared to manage the country.

Christina.

I don't think you can deny that I did my work here competently.

Anne.

You're a wonderful housekeeper.

Christina.

I have common sense and a talent for organisation. [*Pursing her lips.*] It breaks my heart to see the way certain things are done here now.

Anne.

You must remember Violet is very young.

Christina.

Much too young to be a suitable wife for Arthur.

Anne.

He seems to be very well satisfied, and after all he is the person most concerned.

Christina.

I know. His infatuation is—blind, don't you think?

Anne.

[*Coolly.*] I think it's very delightful to see two people so much in love with one another.

Christina.

D'you know that I used to be fearfully jealous of you, Anne?

Anne.

[*Amused.*] I know that you thoroughly disliked me, Christina. You didn't trouble to hide it.

Christina.

I was always afraid that Arthur would marry you. I didn't want to be turned out of this house. I suppose you think that's horrid of me.

Anne.

No, I think it's very natural.

Christina.

I didn't see why Arthur should marry. I gave him all the comforts of home life. And I thought it would interfere with his work. Of course

I knew that he liked you. I suffered agonies when he used to go and dine with you quietly. [*With a sniff.*] He said it rested him.

Anne.

Perhaps it did. Did you grudge him that?

Christina.

I knew you were desperately in love with him.

Anne.

Need you throw that in my face now? Really, I haven't deserved it.

Christina.

My dear, I wish he had married you. It never struck me he'd marry a girl twenty years younger than himself.

Anne.

He never looked upon me as anything but a friend. I don't suppose it occurred to him for an instant that my feeling might possibly be different.

Christina.

It was stupid of me. I ought to have given him a hint.

Anne.

[*With a smile.*] You took care not to do that, Christina. Perhaps you knew that was all it wanted.

Christina.

[*Reflectively.*] I don't think he's treated you very well.

Anne.

Nonsense. A man isn't obliged to marry a woman just because she's in love with him. I don't see why loving should give one a claim on the person one loves.

Christina.

You would have made him a splendid wife.

54

Anne.

So will Violet, my dear. Most men have the wives they deserve.

Christina.

I marvel at your kindness to her. You're so tolerant and sympathetic, one would never imagine she's robbed you of what you wanted most in the world.

Anne.

I shouldn't respect myself very much if I bore her the shadow of a grudge. I'm so glad that she's sweet and charming and ingenuous; it makes it very easy to be fond of her.

Christina.

I know. I wanted to dislike her. But I can't really. There is something about her which disarms one.

Anne.

Isn't it lucky? It's a difficult position. That irresistible charm of hers will make everything possible. After all, you and I can agree in that we both want Arthur to be happy.

Christina.

I wonder if there's much chance of that.

[Anne *looks at her for a moment inquiringly, and* Christina *coolly returns the stare.*]

Anne.

Why did you come here this afternoon, Christina?

Christina.

[*With a faint smile.*] Why did you take so much trouble to get your brother moved to Paris?

Anne.

Good heavens, I told you this morning.

Christina.

D'you think we need make pretences with one another?

Anne.

I don't think I quite understand.

Christina.

Don't you? You wanted Ronny to leave Egypt because you know he's in love with Violet.

[*For a moment* Anne *is a little taken aback, but she quickly recovers herself.*]

Anne.

He's very susceptible. He's always falling in and out of love. I had noticed that he was attracted, and I confess I thought it better to put him out of harm's way.

Christina.

How cunning you are, Anne! You won't admit anything till you're quite certain the person you're talking to knows it. You know as well as I do that Violet is just as much in love with him.

Anne.

[*Much disturbed.*] Christina, what are you going to do? How could I help knowing? You've only got to see the way they look at one another. They're sick with love.

Christina.

What did Arthur expect? I've never seen a couple more admirably suited to one another.

Anne.

I thought no one knew but me till this morning, when you were talking to Arthur. Then I thought you must know too. My heart was in my mouth, I was afraid you were going to tell him. But you didn't, and I thought I'd been mistaken.

Christina.

You didn't give me credit for very nice feeling, Anne. Because I didn't act like a perfect beast you thought I must be a perfect fool.

Anne.

I know how devoted you are to your son. I didn't believe you'd stick at anything when his interests were at stake. I'm sorry, Christina.

Christina.

Pray don't apologise. I didn't know it myself. It was on the tip of my tongue to tell Arthur, but I simply couldn't. I couldn't do anything so shabby.

Anne.

Oh, Christina, we mustn't ever let him know, we can't make him so miserable. It would break his heart.

Christina.

Well, what is to be done?

Anne.

Heaven knows. I've been racking my brains. I can think of nothing. I'd arranged everything so beautifully. And now I'm helpless. I thought even of going to Ronny and asking him to refuse any job that will keep him here. But Arthur looks upon it as so important. He'll insist on Ronny's accepting unless his reasons for going are— what's the word I want?

Christina.

Irrefutable. It seems very hard that my boy should be done out of such a splendid chance by Ronny. Except for your brother I'm sure Arthur would give it to Henry.

Anne.

[*Diplomatically.*] I know he has the highest opinion of Henry's abilities.

Christina.

You can't expect me to sit still and let things go on.

Anne.

Arthur is perfectly unconscious. He thinks Violet is as much in love with him as he is with her. You couldn't be so cruel as to hint anything to him.

Christina.

How you adore him, Anne! You may set your mind at rest. I'm not going to say a word to Arthur. I'm going to speak to Violet.

Anne.

[*Frightened.*] What are you going to say?

Christina.

I'm going to ask her to do all she can to persuade Arthur to give Henry the job. And then Ronny can go to Paris.

Anne.

You're not going to tell her you know?

Christina.

[*Deliberately.*] If it's necessary she must make Ronny refuse the appointment. He must invent some excuse that Arthur will accept.

Anne.

But it's blackmail.

Christina.

I don't care what it is.

[Violet *comes in. She wears an afternoon gown, picturesque and simple, yet elegant enough for the visit she has been paying. She has a large hat, which she presently removes.*]

Anne.

Here is Violet.

Violet.

Oh, you poor people, haven't you had any tea?

Anne.

I thought we'd wait till you came back. It'll come at once now.

Violet.

How are you, Christina? How is Henry? [*They kiss one another.*] I've not seen him for days.

Christina.

He's coming to fetch me presently.

Violet.

I shall tell him he neglects me. He's the only one of my in-laws I'm not a little afraid of.

Christina.

He's a good boy.

Violet.

He has a good mother. I thought it would be such fun having a nephew several years older than myself, but he won't treat me as an aunt. He will call me Violet. I tell him he ought to be more respectful.

[*Meanwhile* Servants *have brought the tea.*]

Christina.

What have you been doing this afternoon?

Violet.

Oh, I went to see the Khedive's mother. She made me eat seventeen different things and I feel exactly like a boa-constrictor. [*Looking at the cakes and scones.*] I'm afraid there's not a very nice tea.

                                    Christina.

So I notice.

                                    Violet.

[*With a smile.*] I suppose I couldn't persuade you to pour it out.

                                    Christina.

[*Gratified.*] Certainly, if you wish it.

[*She sits down in front of the teapot and pours out cups of tea.* Arthur *comes in.*]

                                    Arthur.

Hulloa, Christina, are you pouring out the tea?

                                    Christina.

Violet asked me to.

                                    Violet.

If only I weren't here it would be quite like old times.

                                    Arthur.

I understand you want to see me, Violet.

                                    Violet.

Oh, I hope you haven't come out here on purpose. I sent the message that I wished to have a word with you when convenient, but I didn't want to hurry you. I was quite prepared to go to you.

                                    Arthur.

That sounds very formidable. I had a few minutes to spare while some letters were being prepared for me to sign. But in any case I'm always at your service.

                                    Violet.

The Khedive's mother has asked me to talk to you about a man called Abdul Said.

Arthur.

Oh!

Violet.

She thought if I put the circumstances before you....

Arthur.

[*Interrupting.*] What has he got to do with her?

Violet.

He's been employed for years on an estate of hers up the Nile. His mother was one of her maids. It appears she gave her a dowry when she married.

Arthur.

[*Smiling.*] I see. I gathered that Abdul Said had powerful influence somewhere or other.

Christina.

Who is this man, Arthur?

Arthur.

He's been sentenced to death for murder. It was a perfectly clear case, but there was a lot of perjury and we had some difficulty in getting a conviction. What has the Princess asked you to do?

Violet.

She explained the whole thing to me, and then she asked if I wouldn't intercede with you. I promised to do everything I could.

Arthur.

You shouldn't have done that. The old lady knows quite well an affair of this sort is no business of yours. I wish you'd told her so.

Violet.

Arthur, what could I do? His wife was there, and his mother. If

61

you'd seen them.... I couldn't bear to look at their misery and do nothing. I said I was sure that when you knew all the facts you'd reprieve the man.

Arthur.

It's not in my power to do anything of the sort. The prerogative of mercy is with the Khedive.

Violet.

I know, but if you advise him to exercise it he will. He's only too anxious to, but he won't move without your advice.

Arthur.

It's monstrous of the Princess to try and make use of you in this way. She prepared a complete trap for you.

Anne.

What did the man do exactly?

Arthur.

It's rather a peculiar case. Abdul Said had a difference of opinion with an Armenian merchant and shortly after his only son fell ill and died. He took it into his head that the Armenian had cast the evil eye on him, and he took his gun, waited for his opportunity, and shot the Armenian dead. The man isn't a criminal in the ordinary sense of the word, but we can't afford to make exceptions. If we did there'd be a crop of murders with the same excuse. I looked into the case this morning and I see no reason to advise the Khedive to interfere with the course of justice.

Violet.

This morning? When you came in to luncheon full of spirits, laughing and chaffing, had you just sent a man to his death? How horribly callous!

Arthur.

I'm sorry you should think that. I give every matter my closest attention, and when I've settled it to the best of my ability I put it out of my mind. I think it would be just as unwise to let it affect me as for a doctor to let himself be affected by his patients' sufferings.

Violet.

It seems to me horrible to slaughter that wretched man because he's ignorant and simple-minded. Don't you see that for yourself?

Arthur.

I'm afraid I'm not here to interpret the law according to my feelings but according to its own spirit.

Violet.

It's easy to talk like that when you haven't got any feeling one way or the other. Don't you realise the misery of that man condemned to die for what he honestly thought was a mere act of justice? I wish you'd seen the agony of those poor women. And now they're more or less happy because I promised to help them. The Princess told them I had influence with you. If she only knew!

Arthur.

You should never have been put in such a position. It was grossly unfair. I'll take care that nothing of the sort occurs again.

Violet.

D'you mean to say you'll do nothing? Won't you even go into the matter again—with a little sympathy?

Arthur.

I can't!

Violet.

It's the first thing I've ever asked you, Arthur.

Arthur.

I know. I'm only sorry that I must refuse you.

Violet.

This is the first sentence of death in Egypt since our marriage. Don't you know what it would mean to me to think I'd saved a man's life? The Khedive is waiting to sign the reprieve. It only requires a word from you. Won't you say it? I feel that the gratitude of these poor women may be like a blessing on us.

Arthur.

My dear, I think my duty is very clear. I must do it.

Violet.

It's clear because all that grief means nothing to you. What do you care if a man is hanged whom you've never even seen? I wonder if you'd find it so easy to do your duty in a matter that affected you. If it meant misery or happiness to you. It's easy to do one's duty when one doesn't care.

Arthur.

You're quite right. That is the test: if one can do one's duty when it means the loss of all one holds dear and valuable in the world.

Violet.

I hope you'll never be put to it.

Arthur.

[*With a chuckle.*] My dear, you say that as though you hoped precisely the contrary.

Violet.

Must I write to the Princess and say I was entirely mistaken, and I have no more influence over you than a tripper at Shepheard's Hotel?

Arthur.

I'd sooner you didn't write to her at all. I will have a message conveyed which you may be sure will save you from any humiliation.

Violet.

[*Icily.*] I'm afraid you have a lot of business; you mustn't let me keep you.

64

[*He looks at her reflectively for a moment and then goes out. There is an awkward silence.*]

Violet.

Those good people we had to luncheon to-day would be amused to see what the power amounts to that they congratulated me on.

Christina.

There's very little that Arthur would refuse you. He'd do practically anything in the world to please you.

Violet.

It'll be a long time before I ask him to do anything else.

Christina.

Don't say that, Violet. Because I came here to-day on purpose to ask you to use your influence with him.

Violet.

You see how much I have.

Christina.

That was a matter of principle. Men are always funny about principles. You can never get them to understand that circumstances alter cases.

Violet.

Arthur looks upon me as a child. After all, it's not my fault that I'm twenty years younger than he is.

Christina.

I want your help so badly, Violet. And you know, the fact that Arthur has just refused to do something for you is just the reason that will make him anxious to do anything you ask now.

Violet.

I don't want to expose myself to the humiliation of another refusal.

Christina.

It's so important to me. It may mean all the difference to Henry's future.

Violet.

[*With a change of manner, charmingly.*] Oh! I'd love to do anything I could for Henry.

Christina.

The Khedive has asked Arthur for an English secretary. It seems to me that Henry has every possible qualification, but you know what Arthur is; he's terrified of the least suspicion of favouring his friends and relations.

Violet.

My dear Christina, what can I do? Arthur would merely tell me to mind my own business.

Christina.

He wants to give the post to Ronald Parry....

Violet.

[*Quickly.*] Ronny? But Ronny's going to Paris. It's all arranged.

Christina.

It was. But Arthur thinks it essential that he should stay in Egypt.

Violet.

Did you know this, Anne?

Anne.

Not till just now.

Violet.

Does Ronny know?

Anne.

I don't think so.

66

[Violet *is aghast. She does all she can to hide her agitation. The two* *women watch her*, Christina *with cold curiosity*, Anne *with* *embarrassment.*]

Violet.

I'm ... I'm awfully surprised. It's only an hour or two ago that Ronny and I bade one another a pathetic farewell.

Christina.

Really? But there was never any talk of his going till the day after to-morrow. You were in a great hurry with your leave-takings.

Violet.

I thought he'd be busy packing and that I mightn't have another chance.

Christina.

You've been so intimate, I'm sure he would have been able to snatch a moment to say good-bye to you and Arthur before his train started.

[Violet *does not quite know what this speech means. She gives* Christina *a look.* Anne *comes to the rescue quickly.*]

Anne.

Ronny has been acting as Violet's secretary to a certain extent. I expect they had all sorts of little secrets together that they wanted to discuss in private.

Christina.

Of course. That's very natural. [*With great friendliness.*] If I thought I were robbing you of anyone who was indispensable to you I wouldn't ask you to put in a good word for Henry. But, of course, if Ronald became the Khedive's secretary he couldn't exactly continue to write letters and pay bills for you, could he?

Violet.

I'm rather taken aback. I'd got it fixed in my head that Ronny was going.

Christina.

I can promise you that in helping Henry you're not doing any harm to Ronald. Anne is very anxious that he should leave Egypt. Isn't that so?

Anne.

In a way. Henry is proposing to spend the rest of his official life in Egypt. An appointment like this is naturally more important to him than it would be to Ronny, who is by way of being a bird of passage.

Christina.

Exactly. Ronny has had his experience here. If he stayed longer it would only be waste of time. Anne naturally wants to have him near her. I daresay she's a little afraid of his getting into mischief here.

Anne.

I don't know about that, Christina.

Christina.

My dear, you know how susceptible he is. There's always the possibility that he'll fall in love with someone who isn't very desirable.

Violet.

I've got an awful headache.

Christina.

Why don't you take a little aspirin? I'm quite sure that if you set your mind to it you can persuade Arthur to give the job to Henry. And that would settle everything.

Violet.

And if I can't persuade him?

Christina.

Then you must put it to Ronny.

Violet.

I?

Christina.

You see, if he refused the appointment and left Egypt, then I'm convinced Arthur would accept Henry.

Violet.

Why should I put it to Ronny?

Christina.

[*Pleasantly.*] You've been so very friendly, haven't you? If you suggested to him that ... he's standing in Henry's way....

Violet.

I should have thought it was for Anne to do that.

Christina.

How simple-minded you are! A man will often do for a pretty woman what he won't do for his sister.

Violet.

You want me to make him go?

Christina.

Don't you think yourself that would be the very best thing ... for all parties?

[Violet *and* Christina *look steadily at one another.* Violet *sinks her eyes. She knows that* Christina *is aware of her love. She is terrified.* Ronald *comes in. He is in the highest spirits.*]

Ronny.

I've been sent to have a cup of tea. Sir Arthur is coming along in a minute. I've got some news. I'm staying in Egypt. Isn't it splendid?

[Violet *gives a little gasp.*]

Violet.

Is it settled then?

Ronny.

Did you know? I thought it would be a surprise.

Violet.

No. I've just heard.

Ronny.

Isn't it magnificent?

Christina.

You're very changeable. It's only a few months ago that you were constantly telling Henry you'd had enough of the country.

Ronny.

Never. I love it. I should like to stay here all my life.

Christina.

Fancy that!

Ronny.

[*Addressing himself to* Violet.] It would be madness to leave a place where you're so happy, wouldn't it? I feel so intensely alive here. It's a wonderful country. One lives every minute of the day.

Christina.

You're so enthusiastic. One would almost think you'd fallen in love.

Violet.

Ronny is naturally enthusiastic.

Ronny.

[*To* Christina.] And why shouldn't I have fallen in love?

70

Christina.

Won't you tell us who with?

Ronny.

[*With a chuckle.*] I was only joking. Isn't it enough to have a splendid job in a country where there's so much hope? Sir Arthur has given me a marvellous opportunity. It'll be my fault if I don't make the most of it.

Christina.

[*Dryly.*] Shall I give you a cup of tea?

Ronny.

[*Chaffing her.*] D'you think I want calming down? I feel like a prisoner who was going to be hanged and has just had a free pardon. I don't want to be calmed down. I want to revel in my freedom.

Christina.

All that means, I take it, that you don't want tea.

Ronny.

It's no good trying to snub me. I'm unsnubable to-day. You haven't congratulated me, Anne.

Anne.

My dear, you've been talking nineteen to the dozen. I've not had the chance to get a word in edgeways.

Ronny.

[*To* Violet.] Will you put my name back on your list for that dinner? It would have broken my heart to miss it.

Violet.

Your official position rather alters things, doesn't it? I would never dare to ask you now just to make an even number.

Ronny.

Oh, well, I'm sending out the invitations. I shall write a formal letter to myself, explaining the circumstances, and I daresay I shall see my way to accept.

Christina.

Dear Ronald, you might be eighteen.

[Arthur *comes in with* Henry Pritchard. *This is* Christina's *son, a pleasant, clean young man, but in no way remarkable.*]

Arthur.

Henry tells me he's come to fetch you away, Christina.

Christina.

So you lose not a moment in bringing him here.

Arthur.

Really, Christina, you do me an injustice. I can't bear to think you should be parted from your precious boy an instant longer than necessary.

Henry.

[*Shaking hands with* Violet.] How is my stately aunt?

Violet.

Merry and bright, thank you.

Henry.

You know I'm having a birthday soon, don't you?

Violet.

What of it?

Henry.

I've always been given to understand that aunts give their nephews ten shillings on their birthday.

Violet.

Do they? I am glad. I'd love to press ten shillings into your willing hand.

Henry.

Halloa, Ronny. Lucky devil. I congratulate you.

Ronny.

That's awfully good of you, old man.

Arthur.

On what? Christina!

Christina.

I told Henry. I didn't think it would matter, I thought it better that he should know.

Henry.

I say, Uncle Arthur, I'm afraid mother has been giving you a rotten time. It's not my fault, you know.

Arthur.

What isn't?

Henry.

Well, when mother told me at luncheon that the Khedive had applied for an English secretary, I saw by the beady look in her eye that if I didn't get the job she was going to make things unpleasant for somebody.

Christina.

Really, Henry, I don't know what you mean.

Henry.

Well, mother, you're an old dear....

Christina.

Not so old either.

Arthur.

Certainly not, Henry. Let us have none of your nonsense.

Henry.

But you know perfectly well that you'd cheerfully bring the British Empire tumbling about our ears if you could get me a good fat billet by doing so.

Arthur.

Out of the mouths of babes and sucklings....

Christina.

You've got no right to say that, Henry. I've never asked anything for you that it wasn't practically your right to have.

Henry.

Well, mother, between you and me I don't mind telling you that Ronny is much more suited to this particular job than I am. Only a perfect fool would have hesitated, and for the honour of the family we can't suspect Uncle Arthur of being that.

Arthur.

You see what comes of bringing up a boy properly, Christina; you've made him a decent fellow in spite of yourself.

Christina.

You're a tiresome creature, Henry, but I'm attached to you. You may kiss me.

Henry.

Come along, Mother. I'm not going to kiss you in public.

74

Christina.

[*Getting up.*] Well, good-bye, Violet. Don't forget our little conversation, will you?

Violet.

Good-bye. Good-bye, Henry.

Christina.

[*To* Anne.] Why don't you come for a little drive with us? It's such a beautiful evening.

Anne.

Will you take me? I think I'd like it. It won't take me a minute to put on my hat.

[*She gets up. They start to walk towards the house.*]

Christina.

[*Putting up her cheek.*] Good-bye, Arthur.

Arthur.

Oh, I'll just come along and put you in your carriage. You shan't say that I don't treat you with the ceremony due to your importance.

[*They saunter off.* Violet *and* Ronny *are left alone.*]

Violet.

You're coming back, Arthur?

Arthur.

Oh, yes, in a minute. [*Exit.*]

Ronny.

[*Under his breath.*] Violet.

Violet.

Be quiet.

Ronny.

Isn't it ripping? I could hardly prevent myself from letting them see how much I loved you.

Violet.

You didn't. Christina suspected before and now you've told her in plain words.

Ronny.

[*Gaily.*] That's only your fancy. You think because it's plain to you it must be plain to anybody else.

Violet.

I've never before had anything to hide. D'you think I like it?

Ronny.

And even if she does know, what does it matter? It does her no harm.... And how could anyone help loving you?

Violet.

[*Quickly.*] Take care what you say.

Ronny.

No one can hear. To look at us anyone would think we were discussing the political situation.

Violet.

You're cunning, Ronny.

Ronny.

I love you. I love you. I love you.

Violet.

For God's sake don't keep on saying it. I'm so ashamed.

Ronny.

[*Astonished.*] What about?

Violet.

Just now, this afternoon, I would never have said what I did only I thought you were going. I wasn't myself then, Ronny. I ought never to have....

Ronny.

Thank God you did. You can't grudge me the happiness you gave me. You can't take it away from me now. I know you love me. I hold the sun and the moon in my hands and all the stars of heaven.

Violet.

[*Desperately.*] What are we going to do? Oh, it's not fair to me.

Ronny.

It's done now. You can't unsay it. Each time I look at you I shall remember. I've held you in my arms and kissed your lips. You can never take that away from me. And I needn't go. I shall see you constantly. Oh, I'm so happy.

[*She walks up and down for a moment, trying to control herself, then she makes up her mind: she stops and faces him.*]

Violet.

I want you to go, Ronny. I want you to make some excuse and refuse the appointment here.

Ronny.

No, I can't leave you now.

Violet.

I beseech you to go.

Ronny.

Do you want me to?

Violet.

Yes.

Ronny.

Give me your hand, then.

Violet.

Why?

Ronny.

Give me your hand. [*She gives it him and he holds it.*] Say you love me, Violet.

Violet.

No.

Ronny.

How cold your hand is!

Violet.

Let me go.

Ronny.

D'you really want me to go?

Violet.

You know I don't. I adore you. It'll kill me if you go. [*He bends down and passionately kisses her hand.*] Ronny, Ronny, don't! What are you doing? [*She tears her hand away. She is trembling with emotion. He is white and cold with passion. They sit opposite one another for a while in silence.*] What a punishment! When you told me this afternoon that you loved me I thought I'd never been happy in my life before, and though it tore my heart to think that you must go I felt—oh, I don't know—as though my joy was so overwhelming, there was no room in my heart for anything else. And now I'm wretched, wretched.

Ronny.

But why? Darling! My darling, we were going to be parted, and now we're going to be together. Can anything matter beside that?

Violet.

It's all so hopeless.

Ronny.

It needn't be.

Violet.

How can it be anything else?

Ronny.

I don't love you for a day or a week, Violet; I love you for always.

Violet.

Whatever happens, I'm going to try to do my duty to Arthur.

Ronny.

I'm not seeking to prevent you. What am I asking for? I only want to see you. I want to know that I'm close to you. I want to touch your hand. I want to think of you. What harm can that do you?

Violet.

If I were my own mistress I could laugh and let you do as you choose. But I'm not. I'm bound to you hand and foot. It's torture to me. And the worst of it is I love my bonds. I can't wish to be without them. I'm at your mercy, Ronny. I love you.

Ronny.

Oh, but that's enough for me. I swear to you I don't want you to do anything that you'll ever regret.

Violet.

If it could only be taken out of our hands. If something would only happen.

Ronny.

What can happen?

79

Violet.

Perhaps the Khedive will change his mind. Perhaps the Foreign Office will say you must go to Paris.

Ronny.

Would you be pleased? Violet, I want so little from you. How can it hurt you to give me that? Let us give ourselves a chance to be happy.

Violet.

We shall never be happy. Never. The only thing we can do is to part, and I can't let you go. I can't. I can't. It's asking too much of me.

Ronny.

I love you with all my heart and soul. I didn't know it was possible to love anyone as I love you.

[Arthur *is heard gaily whistling to himself.*]

Violet.

There's Arthur!

Ronny.

[*Quickly.*] Shall I go?

Violet.

Yes. No. Have we got to hide ourselves? Has it come to that already? Oh, I hate myself.

[Arthur *comes in.*]

Violet.

[*Brightly.*] You're very gay this afternoon, Arthur. One doesn't often hear you whistle.

Arthur.

D'you think it's unbecoming to my years or to my dignity?

80

Violet.

Shall I give you a cup of tea?

Arthur.

To tell you the honest truth that is what I came here for.

Violet.

And I was flattering myself it was for the pleasure of my company.

Arthur.

Ronny, will you find out if it would be convenient for the Khedive to see me at eleven o'clock to-morrow?

Ronny.

Very good, sir.

[*He goes out.*]

Violet.

What have you to see the Khedive about—if it isn't a secret?

Arthur.

Not at all. I'm merely going to place before him Ronny's name.

Violet.

Then the matter's not definitely settled yet?

Arthur.

Not formally. I've not had the reply yet to my telegram to the Foreign Office, and I've not had the Khedive's acceptance of my suggestion.

Violet.

But supposing the Foreign Office say they think he'd better go to Paris after all?

Arthur.

I think it's most unlikely. They know by now that the man on the spot is the best judge of the circumstances, and I've accustomed them to giving me a free hand.

Violet.

And you think the Khedive will raise no objection?

Arthur.

He knows Ronny a little and likes him. I think he'll be delighted with my choice.

[*There is a pause.* Arthur *drinks his tea. There is no sign that he is conscious of* Violet's *agitation. She is tortured by indecision.*]

Violet.

Arthur, I'm sorry if I was cross just now about Abdul Said. It was stupid of me to interfere with something that wasn't my business.

Arthur.

Oh, my dear, don't say that. I'm sorry I couldn't do what you wanted.

Violet.

I made myself needlessly disagreeable. Will you forgive me?

Arthur.

Darling, don't reproach yourself. That's more than I can bear. There's nothing to forgive.

Violet.

I owe so much to you. I hate to think that I was horrid.

Arthur.

You don't owe anything to me at all. And you're incapable of being horrid.

[*He seizes her hands and is about to kiss them, when she draws them abruptly away.*]

Violet.

No, don't kiss my hands.

Arthur.

Why not?

[*He is surprised. For an instant she is taken aback. He looks at her hands and she withdraws them as though he could see on them the kisses which* Ronny, *a few minutes before, had pressed on them.*]

Violet.

[*With the faintest laugh of embarrassment.*] If you want to kiss me I prefer you to kiss my cheeks.

Arthur.

That is evidently what they're made for.

[*He does not attempt to kiss them. She gives him a quick glance and looks away.*]

Violet.

Arthur, I'm afraid Christina will be awfully disappointed at Henry's not getting that job.

Arthur.

Let us hope she will bear her disappointment with as much fortitude as I do.

Violet.

I don't think she's entirely given up hope that you will change your mind.

Arthur.

[*With a chuckle.*] I'm sure of that. I don't expect to have much peace till the matter is officially settled. That is why I mean to settle it quickly.

Violet.

What is your objection to Henry?

Arthur.

None. He's not such a good man as Ronald Parry, that's all.

Violet.

The last time there was a good job going Henry just missed getting it.

Arthur.

Henry is one of those men who would do very well for a job if there weren't always somebody just a little bit better applying at the same time.

Violet.

Christina thinks you're so anxious not to favour him because he's your nephew that you are positively biassed against him.

Arthur.

Christina, like the majority of her sex, has an unerring eye for the discreditable motive.

Violet.

She blames me because you won't help Henry. She thinks it's because I'm jealous of her.

Arthur.

How exactly like her! The best mother and the most unreasonable woman I've ever known.

Violet.

[*Forcing the words out.*] It would be a great pleasure to me if you could change your mind and let Henry have the post instead of Ronald Parry.

Arthur.

Oh, my dear, don't ask me to do that. You know how I hate refusing to do anything you wish.

Violet.

Anne is so anxious that Ronny should go to Paris. He's made all his preparations, don't you think you might just as well let him go?

Arthur.

I'm afraid I don't. I want him here.

Violet.

It would be such a joy to me if I could go and tell Christina that you'd consented. It would make such a difference to me, you see. I want her to be fond of me, and I know she'd never forget if I'd been able to do her a good turn like that. Oh, Arthur, won't you?

Arthur.

Darling, I'm afraid I can't.

Violet.

I promise I'll never ask you anything again as long as I live if you'll only do this for me. It means so much to me. You don't know how much.

Arthur.

I can't, Violet.

Violet.

Won't you talk it over with Anne?

Arthur.

To tell you the truth I don't think it's any business of hers.

Violet.

[*Hesitatingly.*] Is it due to her influence that Ronald was appointed to Paris?

Arthur.

Why?

Violet.

I want to know. If she's been pulling strings to get him moved I suppose it's for some reason. He was very comfortable here. It's not often you find a secretary who exactly suits you.

Arthur.

Well, yes, it was her doing. She tells me she doesn't mean to come to Egypt so much as in the past and wants her brother nearer to her.

Violet.

If she wants to see much of her brother she let him choose rather an unfortunate profession.... I wonder she didn't tell you the truth.

Arthur.

[*Quickly.*] I'm convinced she did. I thought her explanation very natural. I'm sorry it's necessary for me to interfere with her plans.

Violet.

I'm sure she wouldn't mind my telling you why she's so anxious Ronny should leave Egypt. She thinks he's in love with a married woman and it seems desirable to get him away. Perhaps she didn't want to tell you. I fancy she's been very uneasy about it.

Arthur.

I daresay it's only a momentary infatuation. Let us hope he will get over it quickly. I can't lose a useful public servant because he happens to have formed an unfortunate attachment.

Violet.

I'm afraid I'm not explaining myself very well. Ronny is desperately in love. There's no other way of putting it. You *must* let him go. After all, you're very fond of him, you've known him since he was a small boy; it isn't as though he were a stray young man sent you by the Foreign Office. You can't be entirely indifferent to him. Perhaps his welfare is at stake. Don't you think it's wiser—it's only kind—to send him out of harm's way.

Arthur.

My dear, you know that I—Arthur Little—would do anything to

please you and that I care very much for the happiness of Anne and the welfare of Ronald Parry. But, you see, I'm an official too, and the official can't do all sorts of things that the man would be very glad to.

Violet.

How can you separate the official and the man? The official can't do things that the man disapproves.

Arthur.

Ah! that's a point that has been discussed ever since states came into being. Are the rules of private morality binding on the statesman? In theory most of us answer yes, but in practice very few act on that principle. In this case, darling, it hardly applies. I see no conflict between the man and the official.

Violet.

You think it doesn't really concern you, Arthur?

Arthur.

I've not said that. But I'm not going to let an appeal to my emotions interfere with my judgment. I think I understand the situation. I'm not proposing to change my mind. I shall present Ronny's name to the Khedive to-morrow.

Violet.

D'you think me very stupid, Arthur?

Arthur.

Not at all, darling. Only a clever woman could achieve your beauty.

Violet.

Then doesn't it occur to you that if I've made such a point of Ronny's going it must be for some very good reason?

Arthur.

[*With a quick look at her.*] Don't you think we'd better leave that subject alone, darling?

87

Violet.

I'm afraid you'll think it silly and vain of me to say so, but I think you should know that—that Ronny's in love with me. That is why I want him to go.

Arthur.

It's very natural that he should be in love with you. I'm always surprised that everybody else isn't. I don't see how I can prevent that except by taking you to live in the depths of the Sahara.

Violet.

Don't make light of it, Arthur. It wasn't very easy for me to tell you.

Arthur.

How do you wish me to take it? I can't blame Ronald. He's by way of being a gentleman. I've been good to him. He'll make the best of a bad job.

Violet.

D'you mean to say that it makes no difference to you?

Arthur.

This secretaryship is a stepping-stone to a very important position. You're not going to ask me to rob him of it because he's done something so very natural as to fall in love with the most charming woman in Egypt? I imagine that all my secretaries will fall in love with you. Poor devils, I don't see how they can be expected to help it.

Violet.

You drive me mad. It's so serious, it's so tremendously serious, and you have the heart to make little jokes about it.

Arthur.

[*Gravely.*] Has it ever struck you that flippancy is often the best way of dealing with a serious situation? Sometimes it's really too serious to be taken seriously.

Violet.

What do you mean by that?

Arthur.

Nothing very much. I was excusing myself for my ill-timed jests.

Violet.

You're determined to keep Ronny here?

Arthur.

Quite. [*There is a pause.* Arthur *gets up and puts his hand on her shoulder.*] I don't think there's anything more to say. If you will forgive me I will get back to the office.

Violet.

No, don't go yet, Arthur. There's something more I want to say to you.

Arthur.

Will you allow me to advise you not to? It's so easy to say too much; it's never unwise to say too little. I beseech you not to say anything that we should both of us regret.

Violet.

You think it's unimportant if Ronny loves me, because you trust me implicitly.

Arthur.

Implicitly.

Violet.

Has it never occurred to you that I might be influenced by his love against my will? Do you think it's so very safe?

Arthur.

If I allowed any doubt on that matter to enter my head I should surely be quite unworthy of your affection.

Violet.

Arthur, I don't want to have any secrets from you.

Arthur.

[*Trying to stop her.*] Don't, Violet. I don't want you to go on.

Violet.

I must now.

Arthur.

Oh, my dear, don't you see that things said can never be taken back. We may both know something....

Violet.

[*Interrupting.*] What do you mean?

Arthur.

But so long as we don't tell one another we can ignore it. If certain words pass our lips then the situation is entirely changed.

Violet.

You're frightening me.

Arthur.

I don't wish to do that. Only you can tell me nothing that I don't know. But if you tell me you may do irreparable harm.

Violet.

D'you mean to say you know? Oh, it's impossible. Arthur, Arthur, I can't help it. I must tell you. It burns my heart. I love Ronny with all my body and soul.

[*There is a pause while they look at one another.*]

Arthur.

Did you think I didn't know?

Violet.

Then why did you offer him the job?

Arthur.

I had to.

Violet.

No one could have blamed you if you had suggested Henry.

Arthur.

My dear, I'm paid a very considerable salary. It would surely be taking money under false pretences if I didn't do my work to the best of my ability.

Violet.

It may mean happiness or misery to all three of us.

Arthur.

I must take the risk of that. You see, Ronny is cut out for this particular position. It's only common honesty to give it him.

Violet.

Don't you love me any more?

Arthur.

Don't ask me that, Violet. You know I love you with all my heart.

Violet.

Then I can't understand.

Arthur.

You don't think I want him to stay, do you? When the telegram came from the Foreign Office ordering him to Paris my middle-aged heart simply leapt for joy. Do you think I didn't see all the advantages he had over me? He seemed to have so much to offer you and I so little.

Violet.

Oh, Arthur!

Arthur.

But if he went away I thought presently you'd forget him. I thought if I were very kind to you and tolerant, and if I asked nothing more from you than you were prepared to give I might in time make you feel towards me, not love perhaps, but tenderness and affection. That was all I could hope for, but that would have made me very happy. Then the Khedive asked for an English secretary, and I knew Ronny was the only man for it. You see, I've been at this work so long, the official in me makes decisions almost mechanically.

Violet.

And supposing they break the heart of the man in you?

Arthur.

[*Smiling.*] By a merciful interposition of Providence we all seem to have just enough strength to bear the burdens that are placed on us.

Violet.

D'you think so?

Arthur.

You like the rest of us, Violet.

Violet.

How long have you known I loved him?

Arthur.

Always. I think perhaps I knew before you did.

Violet.

Why didn't you do something?

Arthur.

Will you tell me what there was to do?

92

Violet.

Aren't you angry with us?

Arthur.

I should be a fool to be that. It seems to me so natural, so horribly natural. He's young and nice-looking and cheery. It seems to me now inevitable that you should have fallen in love with him. You might be made for one another.

Violet.

Oh, do you see that?

Arthur.

It had struck you too, had it? I suppose it's obvious to anyone who takes the trouble to think about it. [*She does not answer.*] Haven't you wished with all your heart that you'd met him first? Don't you hate me now because I married you? [*She looks away.*] My dear child, I'm so sorry for you. I've been very grateful for your kindness to me during the last month or two. I've seen you try to be loving to me and affectionate. I've been so anxious to tell you not to force yourself, because I understood and you mustn't be unhappy about me. But I didn't know how. I could only make myself as little troublesome as possible.

Violet.

You've been immensely good to me, Arthur.

Arthur.

That's the least you had a right to expect of me. I did you a great wrong in marrying you. I knew you didn't love me. You were dazzled by the circumstances. You didn't know what marriage was and how irksome it must be unless love makes its constraints sweeter than freedom. But I adored you. I thought love would come. With all my heart I ask you to forgive me.

Violet.

Oh, Arthur, don't talk like that. You know I was so happy to marry you. I thought you wonderful, I was so excited and flattered—I thought that was love. I never knew that love would come like this. If I'd only known what to expect I could have fought against it. It took me unawares. I never had a chance. It wasn't my fault, Arthur.

Arthur.

I'm not blaming you, darling.

Violet.

It would be easier for me if you did.

Arthur.

It's just bad luck. Bad luck? I might have expected it.

Violet.

Still, I'm glad I've told you. I hated having a secret from you. It's better that we should be frank with one another.

Arthur.

If I can help you in any way I'm glad too that you've told me.

Violet.

What is to be done?

Arthur.

There's nothing to be done.

Violet.

Arthur, until to-day Ronny and I have never exchanged a word that anyone might not have heard. I was happy to be with him, I knew he liked me, I was quite satisfied with that. But when I heard that he was going away suddenly everything was changed. I felt I couldn't bear to let him go. Oh, I'm so ashamed, Arthur.

Arthur.

Dear child!

94

Violet.

I don't know how it happened. He told me he loved me. He didn't mean to. Don't think he's been disloyal to you, Arthur. We were both so upset. It was just as much my fault as his. I couldn't help letting him see how much he meant to me. We thought we were never going to see one another again. He took me in his arms and held me in them. I was so happy and so miserable. I never thought life could mean so much.

Arthur.

And just now when you were alone he kissed your hands.

Violet.

How do you know?

Arthur.

When I wanted to kiss them you withdrew them. You couldn't bear that I should touch them. You felt on them still the pressure of his lips.

Violet.

I couldn't help it. He was beside himself with joy because he needn't go. I don't want to love him, Arthur. I want to love you. I've tried so desperately hard.

Arthur.

My dear, one either loves or one doesn't. I'm afraid trying doesn't do much good.

Violet.

If he stays here I shall have to see him constantly. I shan't have a chance to get over it. Oh, I can't. I can't. It's intolerable. Have pity on me.

Arthur.

I'm afraid you'll be very unhappy. But you see, something more than your happiness is at stake. A little while ago you said you wanted to do more for your country than you did. Does it strike you that you can do something for it now?

Violet.

I?

Arthur.

We all want to do great and heroic things, but generally we can only do very modest ones. D'you think we ought to shirk them?

Violet.

I don't understand.

Arthur.

Ronny can be of infinite value here. You can't help your feelings for him. I can't bring myself to blame you. But you are mistress of your words and your actions. What are we to do? You wouldn't wish me to resign when my work here is but half done. We must make the best of the position. Remember that all of us here, you more than most women, because you're my wife, work for the common cause by our lives and the example we set. At all costs we must seem honest, straightforward, and without reproach. And one finds by experience that it's much less trouble to be a thing than only to seem it. There's only one way in which we can avoid reproach and that is by being irreproachable.

Violet.

You mean that it's necessary for the country that Ronny and you should stay here? And if my heart breaks it doesn't matter. I thought I was doing so much in asking you to send him away. Don't you know that with all my heart I wanted him to stay? D'you know what I feel, Arthur? I can't think of anything else. I'm obsessed by a hungry longing for him. Till to-day I could have borne it. But now ... I feel his arms about me every moment, and his kisses on my lips. You can't know the rapture and the torture and the ecstasy that consume me.

Arthur.

Oh, my dear, do you think I don't know what love is?

Violet.

I want to do the right thing, Arthur, but you mustn't ask too much of

96

me. If I've got to treat him as a casual friend, I can't go on seeing him. I can't, Arthur, I can't! If he must stay then let me go.

Arthur.

Never! I think, even if it weren't necessary, I should make him stay now. You and I are not people to run away from danger. After all, we're not obliged to yield to our passions—we can control them if we want to. For your own sake you must stay, Violet.

Violet.

And if I break, I break.

Arthur.

It's only the worthless who are broken by unhappiness. If you have faith and courage and honesty unhappiness can only make you stronger.

Violet.

Have you thought of yourself, Arthur? What will you feel when you see him with me? What will you suspect when you're working in your office and don't know where I am?

Arthur.

I shall know that you are unhappy, and I shall feel the most tender compassion for you.

Violet.

You're exposing me to a temptation that I want with all my heart to yield to. What is there to hold me back? Only the thought that I must do my duty to you. What is there to reward me? Only the idea that perhaps I'm doing a little something for the country.

Arthur.

I put myself in your hands, Violet. I shall never suspect that you can do anything, not that I should reproach you for—I will never reproach you—but that you may reproach yourself for.

[*A pause.*]

Violet.

Just now, when we were talking of Abdul Said, I asked if you could do your duty when it was a matter that affected you, if it meant misery or happiness to you, I said.

Arthur.

My dear, duty is rather a forbidding word. Let us say that I—want to earn my screw.

Violet.

You must have thought me very silly. I said I hoped you'd never be put to the test, and the test had come already, and you never hesitated.

Arthur.

These things are very much a matter of habit, you know.

Violet.

What you can do I can do too, Arthur—if you believe in me.

Arthur.

Of course I believe in you.

Violet.

Then let him stay. I'll do what I can.

[Ronny *comes in.*]

Ronny.

The Khedive was engaged when I rang up. But I left the message and the answer has just come through. He will be pleased to see you, sir, at eleven o'clock.

Arthur.

That will do admirably. Ronny must lunch with us to-morrow, Violet. We'll crack a bottle to celebrate his step!

END OF THE SECOND ACT

ACT III

The scene shows part of the garden and a verandah at the Consular Agent's house. Coloured lanterns are fixed here and there. It is night, and in the distance is seen the blue sky bespangled with stars. At the lack of the verandah are the windows of the house gaily lit. Within a band is heard playing dance-music. Violet is giving a dance. Everyone who appears is magnificently gowned. Violet is wearing all her pearls and diamonds. Arthur has across his shirt front the broad riband of an order. It is the end of the evening. Various people are sealed on the verandah, enjoying the coolness. They are Mr. *and* Mrs. Appleby, Christina *and* Arthur.

Appleby.

Well, my dear, I think it's about time I was taking you back to your hotel.

Arthur.

Oh, nonsense! It's when everybody has gone that a dance really begins to get amusing.

Christina.

That's a pleasant remark to make to your guests.

Mrs. Appleby.

I'm really ashamed to have stayed like this to the bitter end, but I do love to see the young folk enjoying themselves.

Arthur.

Ah! you have learnt how to make the most of advancing years. The solace of old age is to take pleasure in the youth of those who come after us.

Christina.

I don't think you're very polite, Arthur.

Mrs. Appleby.

Bless your heart, I know I'm not so young as I was.

Arthur.

Do you mind?

Mrs. Appleby.

Me? Why should I? I've had my day and I've enjoyed it. It's only fair to give others a chance now.

Christina.

I'm sure you enjoyed your trip up the Nile.

Mrs. Appleby.

Oh, we had a wonderful time.

Arthur.

And what conclusions did you come to, Mr. Appleby? I remember that you were looking for instruction as well as amusement.

Appleby.

I didn't forget what you told me. I just kept my ears open and my mouth shut.

Arthur.

A capital practice, not much favoured by democratic communities.

Appleby.

But I came to one very definite conclusion for all that.

Arthur.

What was it?

100

Appleby.

In fact, I came to two.

Arthur.

That's not so satisfactory—unless they contradicted one another; in which case I venture to suggest that you have grasped at all events the elements of the Egyptian problem.

Appleby.

The first is that you're the right man in the right place.

Arthur.

Christina would never admit that. She has known for many years that she could manage Egypt far better than I do.

Christina.

I don't deny that for a minute. I think on the whole women are more level-headed than men. They're not swayed by emotion. They're more practical. They know that principle must often yield to expediency, and they can do the expedient without surrendering the principle.

Arthur.

You make my head whirl, Christina.

Appleby.

I had the opportunity of seeing a good many different sorts of people. I never heard a reasonable complaint against you. Some of them didn't like you personally, but they looked up to you, and they believed in you. I asked myself how you managed it.

Mrs. Appleby.

I told him that it's because you're human.

Arthur.

Christina thinks it very bad for me to hear pleasant things said of me.

101

Christina.

Christina doesn't know what her brother would do if he hadn't got an affectionate sister to gibe at.

Appleby.

It must be a great satisfaction to you to see the country becoming every year more prosperous and contented.

Arthur.

What was the second conclusion you came to?

Appleby.

I'm coming to that. Most of us are torn asunder as it were by a conflict of duties. This and that urgently needs to be done, and if you put one thing right you put something else wrong. We all want to do for the best, but we don't exactly know what the best is. Now, you've got your duty clearly marked out before you, if you take my meaning; you're young.

Arthur.

Youngish.

Appleby.

You've made a success of your job and of your life. It's not all of us who can say that. My second conclusion is that you must be the happiest man alive.

Mrs. Appleby.

I'm glad he's got that off his chest. He's been dinning it into my ears for the last ten days. My impression is that he fell in love with Lady Little that day he lunched here six weeks ago.

Arthur.

I'm not going to blame him for that. Everybody does.... It was a wise old fellow who said that you must count no man happy till he's dead. [Christina *gives him a look, and puts her hand affectionately on his arm. He quickly withdraws it.*] Here is Violet.

[*She comes in on* Henry Pritchard's *arm and sinks into a chair.*]

Violet.

I'm absolutely exhausted. I feel that in another minute my legs will drop off.

Arthur.

Do take care, darling, that would be so disfiguring.

Violet.

Oh, I'd still dance on the stumps.

Arthur.

When are you going to send that unfortunate band away?

Violet.

Oh, we must have one more dance. After all, it's our last ball of the season. And now that everyone has gone I needn't be dignified any more. There's no one but Henry and Anne and Ronny. We've just had a gorgeous one-step, haven't we, Henry?

Henry.

Gorgeous. You're a ripping dancer.

Violet.

My one accomplishment. [*The band is heard beginning a waltz.*] Good heavens, they've started again. That's Anne, I'm positive. She's been playing the British matron too and now she's having her fling.

Arthur.

You girls, you never grow up.

Henry.

Are you ready for another turn, Violet?

Arthur.

Don't dance any more, darling, you look worn out.

Violet.

Supposing you danced with your mother, Henry. I can see her toes itching inside her black satin slippers.

Christina.

Nonsense! I haven't danced for fifteen years.

Henry.

Come on, mother. Just to show them you know how.

[*He seizes her hand and drags her to her feet.*]

Christina.

I was just as good a dancer as anybody else in my day.

Arthur.

When Christina says that she means she was a great deal better.

Henry.

Come on, mother, or it'll be over before we begin.

Christina.

Don't be rough with me, Henry.

[*They go into the house.*]

Appleby.

We rather fancied ourselves too, Fanny, once upon a time. What d'you say to trying what we can do, my dear?

Mrs. Appleby.

You be quiet, George. Fancy me dancing with my figure!

Appleby.

I don't deny you're plump, but I never did like a scrag. Perhaps it's the last chance we shall ever have.

104

Mrs. Appleby.

What would they say at home if they ever come to hear you and me had been dancing? Really, George, I'm surprised at you.

Arthur.

[*Amused.*] I won't tell.

Appleby.

You know you want to, Fanny. You're only afraid they'll laugh. Come on, or else I shall dance by myself.

Mrs. Appleby.

[*Getting up.*] I see you've quite made up your mind to make a fool of yourself.

[*They go out.* Arthur *watches them, smiling.*]

Arthur.

What good people! It's really a treat to see them together.

Violet.

Mr. Appleby is very enthusiastic about you. He was telling me just now about his trip in Upper Egypt. He's tremendously impressed. He said I ought to be very proud of you.

Arthur.

I can't imagine any remark more calculated to make you dislike me.

[*She gives him a long look and then glances away. When she speaks it is with embarrassment.*]

Violet.

Are you satisfied with me, Arthur?

Arthur.

My dear, what do you mean?

Violet.

Since that afternoon when I told you....

Arthur.

Yes, I know.

Violet.

We've never talked about it. [*Giving him her hand.*] I want to thank you for having been so good to me.

Arthur.

I'm afraid you haven't got much to thank me for. It would have been easier if I'd been able to help you, but I didn't see anything I could do but just sit still and twiddle my thumbs.

Violet.

I've felt your confidence in me and that has been a help. You've never given the slightest sign that anything was changed. You used sometimes to ask me what I'd been doing during the day. Of late you haven't even done that.

Arthur.

I didn't want you to suspect for a moment that your actions were not perfectly free.

Violet.

I know. No one could have been more considerate than you've been. Oh, I've been so unhappy, Arthur. I wouldn't go through the last six weeks for anything in the world.

Arthur.

It's torn my heart to see you so pale and wan. And when, often, I saw you'd been crying I almost lost my head. I didn't know what to do.

Violet.

I couldn't help it if I loved him, Arthur. That wasn't in my power.

106

But all that was in my power I've done. Somehow I've managed not to be alone with him.

Arthur.

Haven't you had any explanation with him?

Violet.

There didn't seem to be anything to explain. D'you think I ought to have told him I didn't love him? I couldn't, Arthur. I couldn't.

Arthur.

My dear! My dear!

Violet.

Once or twice he wrote to me. I knew he would and I'd made up my mind not to read the letters. But when they came I couldn't help myself. I had to read them. I was so wretched and it meant so much to me that he loved me. [Arthur *makes an instinctive movement of pain*.] I didn't mean to say that. Please forgive me.

Arthur.

I think I understand.

Violet.

I didn't answer them.

Arthur.

Did he only write once or twice?

Violet.

That's all. You see, he can't make it out. He thinks I've treated him badly. Oh, I think that's the hardest thing of all. I've seen the misery in his eyes. And there was nothing I could do. I hadn't the courage to tell him. I'm weak. I'm so horribly weak. And when I'm with him alone I.... Oh, it is cruel that I should make him suffer so when he loves me.

107

Arthur.

I don't know what to say to you. It seems cold comfort to say that you must set your hope in the merciful effects of time. Time will ease your pain and his. Perhaps the worst is over already.

Violet.

I hope with all my heart it is. I couldn't have borne any more, Arthur. I'm at the end of my strength.

Arthur.

Dear heart, you're tired physically now. We'll send these people away and you must go to bed.

Violet.

Yes. I'm exhausted. But I want to tell you, Arthur, I think you're right. The worst is over. I'm not suffering quite so much as I did. I find it a little easier not to think of him. When I meet him I can manage to be gay and flippant and indifferent. I'm so glad, Arthur.

Arthur.

You've been very brave. I told you we were all strong enough to bear the burdens that are laid upon us.

Violet.

You mustn't think too well of me. I couldn't have done what I have except for the consciousness of his great love for me. Is that awfully disloyal of me, Arthur?

Arthur.

[*Gravely.*] No, darling.

Violet.

You can understand, can't you? It means so much to me. It's helped me more than anything else in the world. It's the only thing that made these past weeks not intolerable. I'm satisfied to know he loves me. I want nothing more.

[Mr. *and* Mrs. Appleby *come in.* Arthur *immediately assumes a chaffing manner.*]

Arthur.

Why, what's this? You haven't given in already?

Appleby.

The spirit is willing enough, but the flesh is weak.

Mrs. Appleby.

We wouldn't like it talked about at home, but the fact is we got a bit out of breath.

Violet.

Well, sit down a moment and rest yourself.

Mrs. Appleby.

Just a moment if you don't mind, and then we'll be going.

[Christina *appears with* Henry.]

Arthur.

Here is poor Christina in a state of complete mental and physical collapse.

Christina.

Don't be ridiculous, Arthur.

Arthur.

How did you get on?

Henry.

First rate. Only mother won't let herself go. I kept on telling her there's only one thing to do in modern dancing—let all your bones go loose and leave the man to do the rest.

Christina.

[*With a chuckle.*] I think modern dancing is an abandoned pastime. Nothing will induce me to let all my bones go loose.

Henry.

Mother's idea of dancing is to keep herself to herself.

Christina.

[*Looking at him affectionately.*] You're an impudent boy.

Mrs. Appleby.

[*To* Violet.] I do wish I'd seen you dancing with Mr. Parry. He's a wonderful dancer.

Violet.

He does dance well, doesn't he?

Henry.

Haven't you danced with him to-night, Violet?

Violet.

No. He came rather late and my card was filled up. I promised him an extra, but some stuffy old diplomatist came and asked me for a dance, so I gave him Ronny's.

Mrs. Appleby.

It's too bad. It must be a rare sight to see you and Mr. Parry waltzing together.

Violet.

How do you know he dances so well?

Mrs. Appleby.

There were two or three dances at our hotel last week and we saw him then.

Violet.

Oh, I see.

Appleby.

[*With a chuckle.*] I like that young man. When he gets hold of a good thing he freezes on to it.

Violet.

Oh?

Appleby.

There's a young American girl staying at the hotel. She's a Miss Pender. I wonder if you know her?

Violet.

No, I don't think so. We get to know very few of the winter visitors.

Mrs. Appleby.

She's a perfect picture to look at. And a beautiful dancer.

Appleby.

Everyone was looking at them last night. They made a wonderful pair.

Violet.

Do you know this lady, Henry?

Henry.

Yes, I've met her two or three times. She's very pretty.

Appleby.

I don't think anyone else had much of a look in with her.

Henry.

Well, you needn't be disagreeable about it.

Appleby.

As far as I could see she danced with Mr. Parry pretty well all the time.

Mrs. Appleby.

It was a treat to see them together.

Violet.

[*A little uncertainly.*] If one gets hold of a partner who suits one I always think it's better to stick to him.

Mrs. Appleby.

Oh, I don't think it was only that. She's so much in love with him that she can't help showing it.

Henry.

I never saw such a fellow as Ronny. When there is a bit of luck going he always gets it.

Violet.

And is he in love with her too?

Appleby.

Oh, one can't tell that.

Mrs. Appleby.

If he isn't he very soon will be. She's too pretty for any man to resist long.

Arthur.

[*Lightly.*] You know them, the brutes, don't you?

Mrs. Appleby.

Bless their hearts, I don't blame them. What are pretty girls for except to make nice men happy? I was a pretty girl myself once.

Arthur.

And was Mr. Appleby a nice man?

Appleby.

I think I must have been, for you've certainly made me happy, my dear.

112

Mrs. Appleby.

I wish you'd put that in writing, George. I'd like to have a little something like that by me when you've got a bit of a chill on your liver.

Appleby.

H'm, I think bed's the place for you, Fanny. Say good-night to her ladyship and let's be going.

Mrs. Appleby.

Good-night, Lady Little, and thank you so much for asking us. We have enjoyed ourselves.

Violet.

Good-night.

Appleby.

Good-night.

Arthur.

I hope you'll have a pleasant journey home. Lucky people, you'll see the spring in England. When you get back the hedgerows will be just bursting into leaf.

[*The* Applebys *go out.*]

Violet.

How old is this American girl, Henry?

Henry.

Oh, I don't know, about nineteen or twenty.

Violet.

Is she as pretty as they say?

Henry.

Rather.

Violet.

Is she fair?

Henry.

Very. She's got wonderful hair.

Violet.

You've never mentioned her. Do you think Ronny is in love with her?

Henry.

Oh, I don't know about that. She's great fun. And you know, it's always flattering when a pretty girl makes a dead set at you.

[*There is a momentary silence.* Violet *is extremely disturbed by the news that has just reached her.* Arthur *realises that a crisis has come.*]

Christina.

[*In a matter-of-fact way.*] Let us hope that something will come of it. There's no reason why Ronny shouldn't marry. I think men marry much too late nowadays.

[Anne *and* Ronny *appear.*]

Anne.

I'm absolutely ashamed of myself. I half expected to find you'd all gone to bed.

Violet.

[*Smiling.*] Have you been having a jolly dance?

Anne.

Think of having a good band and the whole floor to oneself. By the way, Violet, the band want to know if they can go away.

Violet.

I'm sorry I had to cut your dance, Ronny.

114

Ronny.

It was rotten luck. But I suppose on these occasions small fry like me have to put up with that sort of thing.

Violet.

If you like we'll have a turn now before we send the band away.

Ronny.

I'd love it.

[Arthur *gives a little start and looks at* Violet *curiously.* Anne *is surprised too.*]

Christina.

If you're going to start dancing again we'll go. Henry has to be at his office early in the morning.

Violet.

Good-night, then.

Christina.

[*Kissing her.*] Your dance has been a great success.

Violet.

It's nice of you to say so.

Christina.

[*To* Arthur.] Good-night, dear old thing. God bless and guard you always.

Arthur.

My dear Christina, why this embarrassing emotion?

Christina.

I don't know what we should do if anything happened to you.

Arthur.

Don't be an idiot, my dear; nothing is going to happen to me.

Christina.

[*With a smile.*] I can't get you out of thinking me a perfect fool.

Arthur.

Be off with you, Christina. If you go on finding out things that are not your business I shall have you deported.

Violet.

What has she found out now?

Arthur.

A trifle that we thought it wouldn't hurt the public to know nothing about.

Christina.

[*Shaking hands with* Ronny.] I don't grudge you your job any more. We're all under a debt of gratitude to you.

Ronny.

I had a bit of luck, that's all. It's nothing to make a fuss about.

Arthur.

Go and have your dance, darling. It's really getting very late.

Violet.

[*To* Ronny.] Are you ready?

Ronny.

What shall we make them play?

[*They go out.*]

Christina.

Good-night, Anne.

Anne.

[*Kissing her.*] Good-night, my dear. [*Henry shakes hands with*

Anne *and* Arthur. *He and his mother go out.*] I suppose I mayn't ask what Christina was referring to?

Arthur.

I can't prevent you from asking.

Anne.

But you have no intention of answering. What is the matter, Arthur? You look so deadly white.

Arthur.

Nothing. I'm tired. I had a busy day and now the dance. [*The sound of a waltz is heard.*] Oh, damn that music!

Anne.

Sit down and rest yourself. Why don't you have a smoke! [*Putting her hand on his arm.*] My dear friend.

Arthur.

For God's sake don't pity me.

Anne.

Won't you talk to me frankly? I may be able to help you. In the old days you used to bring your troubles to me, Arthur.

Arthur.

I tell you I'm only tired. What is the use of talking about what can't be helped?

Anne.

You must know that I notice most things that concern your happiness. [*Looking away.*] Why did you imagine I took so much trouble to get Ronny moved to Paris?

Arthur.

I suspected. Ought I to thank you? I'm too miserable and too humiliated.

117

Anne.

Have you heard about a Miss Pender? She's an American girl.

Arthur.

Of course I have. It's my business to know everything that goes on in Cairo.

Anne.

Don't you think that may be the solution?

[Henry *comes in.*]

Arthur.

[*Sharply.*] What d'you want?

Henry.

I beg your pardon. Mother left her fan here.

[*He takes it up from a chair.*]

Arthur.

I thought you'd gone five minutes ago.

Henry.

Oh, we just stood for a moment to look at Ronny and Violet dancing. Upon my soul it's a fair treat.

Arthur.

They make a wonderful couple, don't they?

Henry.

I'm afraid Violet's awfully tired. She's not saying a word and she's as white as a sheet.

Arthur.

I'll send her to bed as soon as they've finished.

Henry.

Good-night.

Arthur.

[*Smiling*.] Good-night, my boy.

[*Exit* Henry.]

Anne.

Is anything the matter?

Arthur.

Tell me about this American girl. She's in love with Ronny, isn't she?

Anne.

Yes, that's obvious.

Arthur.

And he?

Anne.

He's been very unhappy, you know.

Arthur.

[*Almost savagely*.] That is a calamity which I find myself able to bear with patience.

Anne.

And now he's surprised and pleased. I've met her. Poor dear, she did everything to make me like her, because Ronny was my brother. She's awfully pretty. He's not in love with her yet. But I think he may be. He's on the brink and if there were nothing else he'd fall over.

Arthur.

That is what I suspected. You know, Anne, the longer I live the more inexplicable I find human beings. I always thought I was by way of being a fairly decent fellow. I never knew what mean beastliness there was inside me. It would be quite impossible for me to tell you how I hate your brother. I've had to be jolly and affable with him and, by George, I wanted to kill him.

Anne.

Why didn't you let him go? Are you sure it was necessary to give him that job?

Arthur.

Already he's been invaluable.

Anne.

Then one can only hope for the best.

[*There is a moment's pause. When* Arthur *speaks it is at first rather to himself than to* Anne.]

Arthur.

No one knows what I've gone through during the last few months. I've been devoured with jealousy and I knew it would be fatal if I showed Violet the least trace of ill-temper. I kept on saying to myself that it wasn't her fault if she was in love with Ronny. [*Humorously.*] You can't think how devilish hard it is not to resent the fact that somebody doesn't care for you.

Anne.

[*With a chuckle.*] Oh yes, I can.

Arthur.

I knew that almost everything depended on how I acted during these weeks, and the maddening thing was that I could do nothing but sit still and control myself. I saw her miserable and knew that she didn't want my comfort. I've yearned to take her in my arms and I've known she'd *let* me because it was her duty. Those dear good donkeys, the Applebys, told me just now they thought I must be the happiest man alive! Week after week, with an aching heart I've forced myself to be gay and amusing. D'you think I'm amusing, Anne?

Anne.

Sometimes.

Arthur.

The battle has been so unfair. All the dice are loaded against me. He has every advantage over me. But at last I thought I'd won. I thought Violet was getting more resigned. She told me herself just now that the worst was over. And those confounded people must go and upset the applecart. Damn their eyes!

Anne.

Why?

Arthur.

The Applebys told her about Miss Pender. It was very natural. They knew no reason for not repeating the hotel gossip.

Anne.

Was that why she asked Ronny to dance with her?

Arthur.

Yes. It's the crisis. She had the strength to keep him at arm's length when she knew he loved her. What will she do now?

Anne.

You heard what Henry said. They don't seem to be talking to one another.

Arthur.

No.

Anne.

Why did you let them dance together? You might easily have said it was too late and the band must go.

Arthur.

What good would that do? No. I've done nothing to prevent their meeting. I've left them absolute liberty.

Anne.

Do you think it's fair to Violet? You know, women act so much on impulse. The surroundings and the circumstances have so much influence on them. Think of the excitement of dancing, the magic of this wonderful night, and the solitude under these stars. You complain the dice are loaded against you, but now you're double-loading them against yourself.

Arthur.

It tortures me, but I must give them the opportunity to fight the matter out for themselves.

Anne.

Poor child, she's so young.

Arthur.

Too young.

Anne.

Don't say that; it sounds as though you regretted having married her.

Arthur.

Don't you imagine that regret has been tormenting her ever since she found out what love really was? Even though I love her with all my heart I know now that I made a mistake. Do you think you can make anyone love you by constant tenderness, devotion, and kindness?

Anne.

Not a man perhaps. But a woman yes, yes, yes!

Arthur.

Whoever loved that loved not at first sight? I want so tremendously to make her happy, and I've only made her utterly miserable. And there's no way out. It's a pity that a convenient attack of brain fever can't carry me off, but I'm as strong as a horse.

Anne.

You know, Arthur, there's one compensation about the pains of love. While one's suffering from them one feels one will never get over them, but one does, and when they're gone they don't even leave a scar. One looks back and remembers one's torment and marvels that it was possible to suffer like that.

Arthur.

You talk as though you'd had experience.

Anne.

I have.

Arthur.

I always look upon you as so calm and self-controlled.

Anne.

I was desperately in love for years with a man. I should have made him an excellent wife, although it's I as says it. But it never occurred to him for an instant that my feelings were more than friendly. And eventually he married somebody else.

Arthur.

My dear friend, I hate to think of your being unhappy.

Anne.

I'm not. That's why I told you the tragic story. I've got over it so completely that now I have an equal affection both for him and his wife.

Arthur.

D'you know, Anne, at one time I very nearly asked you to marry me?

Anne.

[Gaily.] Oh, what nonsense!

Arthur.

I daresay it's as well I didn't. I should have lost the best friend I've ever had.

123

Anne.

On the other hand, I've lost the satisfaction of refusing the most distinguished man of our day. Why didn't you ask me?

Arthur.

You were such an awfully good friend. I thought we were very well as we were.

Anne.

That isn't the reason, Arthur. You didn't ask me because you didn't love me. If you had you'd have let friendship go hang. [*Seeing that he is not paying any attention to her*.] What's the matter?

Arthur.

The music has stopped.

Anne.

[*With a slight tightening of the lips*.] I'm afraid my concerns don't interest you very much. I was only talking about them to distract you.

Arthur.

Forgive me, but I've got this anguish gnawing at my heart. Anne, when they come back here I want you to come with me for a stroll in the garden.

Anne.

Why? I'm frightfully tired. I think I shall go to bed.

Arthur.

No, do this for me, Anne. I want to give them their chance. It may be the last chance for all of us.

Anne.

[*With a little sigh*.] Very well, I'll do even that for you.

Arthur.

You are a good friend, and I'm a selfish beast.

Anne.

I wish you could have a child, Arthur. That might settle everything.

Arthur.

That is what I look forward to with all my heart. I think she might love her baby's father.

Anne.

Then she'll realise that only you could have been so tolerant and so immensely patient. When she looks back she'll be filled with gratitude.

[Ronny *and* Violet *come in.*]

Violet.

I've told the band they can go.

Arthur.

I don't suppose they wanted telling twice. Did you have a pleasant dance?

Violet.

I was very tired.

Ronny.

It was brutal of me to make you dance so long. I'll say good-night before I'm turned out.

Arthur.

Oh, won't you sit down and have a cigarette before you go? Anne and I were just going to stroll to the end of the garden to have a look at the Nile.

Violet.

Oh.

Anne.

I'm too restless to go to bed just yet.

[Arthur *and* Anne *go out.* Violet *and* Ronny *do not speak for a moment. At first the conversation is quite light.*]

Violet.

What was it that Christina was referring to just now? Had it anything to do with you?

Ronny.

I don't think I'm justified in telling you about it. If Sir Arthur thinks you should know I daresay he'd rather tell you himself.

Violet.

Of course you mustn't tell me if it's a secret.

Ronny.

I'd almost forgotten what a beautiful dancer you were.

Violet.

[*With a smile.*] So soon?

Ronny.

You haven't given me much chance of dancing with you during the last few weeks.

Violet.

I hear there's a girl at the Ghezireh Palace who dances very well. Miss Pender, isn't that her name?

Ronny.

Yes, she's wonderful.

Violet.

I'm told she's charming.

Ronny.

Very.

126

Violet.

I should like to meet her. I wonder whom I know that could bring us together.

Ronny.

[*With a change of tone.*] Why do you speak of her?

Violet.

Is there any reason why I shouldn't?

Ronny.

Do you know that this is the first time I've been quite alone with you for six weeks?

Violet.

[*Still quite lightly.*] It was inevitable that when you ceased being Arthur's private secretary we should see less of one another.

Ronny.

I only welcomed my new job because I thought I shouldn't be utterly parted from you.

Violet.

Don't you think it was better that we shouldn't see too much of one another?

Ronny.

What have I done to you, Violet? Why have you been treating me like this?

Violet.

I'm not conscious that I've treated you differently from what I used.

Ronny.

Why didn't you answer my letters?

Violet.

[*In a low voice.*] I hadn't anything to say.

Ronny.

I wonder if you can imagine what I went through, the eagerness with which I looked forward to a letter from you, just a word or two would have satisfied me, how anxiously I expected each post, and my despair when day after day went by.

Violet.

You ought not to have written to me.

Ronny.

D'you think I could help myself? Have you forgotten that day when we thought we were never going to meet again? If you wanted me to be nothing more than a friend why did you tell me you loved me? Why did you let me kiss you and hold you in my arms?

Violet.

You know quite well. I lost my head. I was foolish. You—you attached too much importance to the emotion of the moment.

Ronny.

Oh, Violet, how can you say that? I know you loved me then. After all, the past can't be undone. I loved you. I know you loved me. We couldn't go back to the time when we were no more than friends.

Violet.

You forget that Arthur is my husband and you owe him everything in the world. We both owe him everything in the world.

Ronny.

No, I don't forget it for a moment. After all, we're straight, both of us, and we could have trusted ourselves. I wanted nothing but to be allowed to love you and to know that you loved me.

Violet.

Do you remember what you said in the first letter you wrote me?

Ronny.

Oh, you can't blame me for that. I'd loved you so long, so passionately. I'd never dared to hope that you cared for me. And when I knew! I never said a tenth part of what I wanted to. I went home and I just wrote all that had filled my heart to overflowing. I wanted you to know how humbly grateful I was for the wonderful happiness you'd given me. I wanted you to know that my soul to its most hidden corners was yours for ever.

Violet.

How *could* I answer it?

Ronny.

You needn't have been afraid of me, Violet. If it displeased you I would never even have told you that I loved you. I would have carried you in my heart like an image of the Blessed Virgin. When we met here or there, though there were a thousand people between us and we never exchanged a word, I should have known that we were the only people in the world, and that somehow, in some strange mystic fashion, I belonged to you and you belonged to me. Oh, Violet, I only wanted a little kindness. Was it so much to ask?

[Violet *is moved to the very depths of her heart. She can scarcely control herself, the pain she suffers seems unendurable; her throat is so dry that she can hardly speak.*]

Violet.

They say that Miss Pender is in love with you. Is it true?

Ronny.

A man's generally a conceited ass when he thinks girls are in love with him.

Violet.

Never mind that. Is it true? Please be frank with me.

Ronny.

Perhaps it is.

Violet.

Would she marry you if you asked her?

Ronny.

I think so.

Violet.

She can't have fallen in love with you without some encouragement.

Ronny.

She plays tennis a good deal and she's very fond of dancing. You know, I was rather wretched. Sometimes you looked at me as though you hated me. You seemed to try and avoid me. I wanted to forget. I didn't know what I'd done to make you treat me so cruelly. It was very pleasant to be with someone who seemed to want me. Everything I did pleased her. She's rather like you. When I was with her I was a little less unhappy. When I found she was in love with me I was touched and I was tremendously grateful.

Violet.

Are you sure you're not in love with her?

Ronny.

Yes, I'm quite sure.

Violet.

But you like her very much, don't you?

Ronny.

Yes, very much.

Violet.

Don't you think if it weren't for me you would be in love with her?

Ronny.

I don't know.

130

Violet.

I'd like you to be frank with me.

Ronny.

[*Unwillingly.*] You don't want my love. She's sweet and kind and tender.

Violet.

I think she might make you very happy.

Ronny.

Who knows?

[*There is a pause.* Violet *forces herself to make the final renunciation. Her fingers move spasmodically in the effort she makes to speak calmly.*]

Violet.

It seems a pity that you should waste your life for nothing. I'm afraid you'll think me a heartless flirt. I'm not that. At the time I feel all I say. But ... I don't quite understand myself. I take a violent fancy to someone, and I lose my head, but somehow it doesn't last. I ... I suppose I'm not capable of any enduring passion. There are people like that, aren't there? It goes just as suddenly as it comes. And when it goes—well, it's gone for ever. I can't understand then what on earth I saw in the man who made my heart go pit-a-pat. I'm dreadfully sorry I caused you so much pain. You took it so much more seriously than I expected. And afterwards I didn't know what to do. You must—you must try to forgive me.

[*There is a long pause.*]

Ronny.

Don't you love me at all now?

Violet.

It's much better that I should tell you the truth, isn't it? even at the risk of hurting your feelings. I'm frightfully ashamed of myself. I'm afraid you'll think me awfully frivolous.

131

Ronny.

Why don't you say it right out?

Violet.

D'you want me to? [*She hesitates, but then takes courage.*] I'm very sorry, dear Ronny, I'm afraid I don't care for you in that way at all.

Ronny.

I'm glad to know.

Violet.

You're not angry with me?

Ronny.

Oh, no, my dear, how can you help it? We're made as we're made.... D'you mind if I go now?

Violet.

Won't you stop and say good-night to Anne?

Ronny.

No, if you don't mind, I'd like to go quickly.

Violet.

Very well. And try to forgive me, Ronny.

Ronny.

Good-night.

[*He takes her hand and they look into one another's eyes.*]

Violet.

Good-night.

[*He goes out.* Violet *clasps her hands to her heart as though to ease its aching.* Anne *and* Arthur *return.*]

132

Anne.

Where is Ronny?

Violet.

He's gone. It was so late. He asked me to say good-night to you.

Anne.

Thank you. It must be very late. I'll say good-night too. [*She bends down and kisses* Violet.] Good-night, Arthur.

Arthur.

Good-night. [*She goes out.* Arthur *sits down. A* Sais *comes in and turns out some of the lights. In the distance is heard the wailing of an Arab song.* Arthur *motions to the* Sais.] Leave these. I'll turn them out myself. [*The* Sais *goes in and turns out all the lights in the lower rooms but one. The light remains now only just round* Arthur *and* Violet. *The Arab song is like a wail of pain.*] That sounds strangely after the waltzes and one-steps that we've heard this evening.

Violet.

It seems to come from very far away.

Arthur.

It seems to wail down the ages from an immeasurable past.

Violet.

What does it say?

Arthur.

I don't know. It must be some old lament.

Violet.

It's heartrending.

Arthur.

Now it stops.

The garden is so silent. It seems to be listening too.

Are you awfully unhappy, Violet?

Awfully.

It breaks my heart that I, who would do anything in the world for you, can do so little to console you.

Had you any idea that Ronny no longer cared for me?

How should I know what his feelings were?

It never occurred to me that he could change. I felt so secure in his love. It never occurred to me that anyone could take him from me.

Did he tell you he didn't care for you any more?

No.

I don't think he's in love with Miss Pender.

I told him that he meant nothing to me any more. I told him that I took fancies and got over them. I made him think I was a silly flirt. And he believed me. If he loved me truly, truly, as he did before, whatever I'd said he'd have known it was incredible. Oh, I wouldn't have believed him if he'd made himself cheap in my eyes.

Arthur.

My poor child.

Violet.

He's not in love with her yet. I know that. He's only pleased and flattered. He's angry with me. If he's angry he *must* love me still. He asked so little. It only needed a word and he would have loved me as much as ever. What have I done? What harm would it have done you? I've sent him away now for good. It's all over and done with. And my heart aches. What shall I do, Arthur?

Arthur.

My dear, have courage. I beseech you to have courage.

Violet.

I suppose it's shameful that we should have loved one another at all. But how could we help it? We're masters of our actions, but how can we command our feelings? After all, our feelings are our own. I don't know what I'm going to do, Arthur. It wasn't so bad till to-night; I could control myself, I thought my pain was growing less.... I long for him with all my soul, and I must let him go. Oh, I hate him. I hate him. If he'd loved me he might have been faithful to me a few short weeks. He wouldn't cause me such cruel pain.

Arthur.

Don't be unjust to him, Violet. I think he fell in love with you without knowing what was happening to him. And when he knew I think he struggled against it as honourably as you did. You know that very little escapes me. I've seen a sort of shyness in him when he was with me, as though he were a little ashamed in my presence. I even felt sorry for him because he felt he was behaving badly to me and he couldn't help himself. He's suffered just as much as you have. It's not very strange that when this girl fell in love with him it should seem to offer a new hope. He was unhappy and she comforted him. Anne says she's rather like you. If ever he loves her perhaps it will be you that he loves in her.

Violet.

Why do you say all this to me?

135

Arthur.

You've been so wretched. I don't want bitterness to come to you now. I can't bear that you should think your first love has been for someone not worthy of it. I think time will heal the wounds which now you think are incurable, but when it does I hope that you will look back on your love as a thing only of beauty.

Violet.

I am a beast, Arthur. I don't deserve anyone to be so good to me as you are.

Arthur.

And there's something else I must tell you.... It appears that various enterprising people have been laying plans to put me out of the way.

Violet.

[*Startled.*] Arthur!

Arthur.

I find that there was a plot to kill me this morning on my way to the review.

Violet.

How awful!

Arthur.

Oh, it's nothing to be alarmed about. We've settled everything without any fuss. Our old friend Osman Pasha is going to spend some time on his country estates for the good of his health, and half a dozen foolish young men are under lock and key. But it might have come off except for Ronny. It was Ronny who saved me.

Violet.

Ronny? Oh, I'm so glad. It makes up a little for the rest.

Arthur.

He did a fine thing. He showed determination and presence of mind.

136

Violet.

Oh, my husband! My dear, dear Arthur!

Arthur.

You're not sorry?

Violet.

I'm glad I've done what I have, Arthur. I've sometimes felt I gave you so little in return for all you've given me. But at least now I've given you all I had to give.

Arthur.

Don't think it will be profitless. To do one's duty sounds a rather cold and cheerless business, but somehow in the end it does give one a queer sort of satisfaction.

Violet.

What should I do if I lost you? It makes me sick with fear.

Arthur.

[*With a tender smile.*] I had an idea you'd be glad I escaped.

Violet.

All I've suffered has been worth while. I've done something for you, haven't I? And even something for England ... I'm so tired.

Arthur.

Why don't you go to bed, darling?

Violet.

No, I don't want to go yet. I'm too tired. Let me stay here a little longer.

Arthur.

Put your feet up.

Violet.

Come and sit close to me, Arthur. I want to be comforted. You're so good and kind to me, Arthur. I'm so glad I have you. You will never fail me.

Arthur.

Never. [*She gives a little shudder.*] What's the matter?

Violet.

I hope he'll marry her quickly. I want to be a good wife to you. I want your love. I want your love so badly.

Arthur.

My dear one.

Violet.

Put your arms round me. I'm so tired.

Arthur.

You're half asleep.... Are you asleep?

[*Her eyes are closed. He kisses her gently. In the distance there is heard again the melancholy wail of a Bedouin love-song.*]

THE END

www.ingramcontent.com/pod-product-compliance
Lightning Source LLC
Chambersburg PA
CBHW020141180626
46810CB00004B/1666